Folk Tales from Japan

-a collection of stories retold

Priyanka Bhandarkar

Ukiyoto Publishing

All global publishing rights are held by

Ukiyoto Publishing

Published in 2024

Content Copyright © Priyanka Bhandarkar

ISBN 9789362691736

All rights reserved.

No part of this publication may be reproduced, transmitted, or stored in a retrieval system, in any form by any means, electronic, mechanical, photocopying, recording or otherwise, without the prior permission of the publisher.

The moral rights of the author have been asserted.

This is a work of fiction. Names, characters, businesses, places, events, locales, and incidents are either the products of the author's imagination or used in a fictitious manner. Any resemblance to actual persons, living or dead, or actual events is purely coincidental.

This book is sold subject to the condition that it shall not by way of trade or otherwise, be lent, resold, hired out or otherwise circulated, without the publisher's prior consent, in any form of binding or cover other than that in which it is published.

www.ukiyoto.com

TO MY FAMILY
For keeping faith in me.

Acknowledgement

I am particularly indebted to the online archives, databases, and community forums that have served as invaluable repositories of information. The curation and annotation work gathered has been instrumental in my research and selection process. The information has been gathered into making these timeless stories accessible to a larger audience in the form of books. These folktales found online have opened up a world of wonder and wisdom to a global plethora of children.

I also wish to acknowledge the support and guidance of my family and friends whose curiosity has helped shape this collection. My vision has been crucial in bringing these digitally sourced folktales to life on a printed page.

The book of folktales would not have been possible without the digital preservation of these precious cultural narratives. I am deeply grateful to the countless individuals in the world who show a generous interest in reading books containing folktales thus reviving the old cultural vibe.

Finally, once again I thank the readers who will loyally engage with these stories. May these tales from the vast online folkloric landscape continue to inspire you, transport you and connect you to the rich cultural tapestry of our world.

Contents

Preface	1
Introduction	2
The Two Frogs	3
The Tongue-Cut Sparrow	7
The Stonecutter	10
The Mirror of Matsuyama	14
The Adventures of Little Peachling	17
My Lord Bag of Rice	19
The Farmer and the Badger	23
The Jellyfish and the Monkey	27
The White Hare and the Crocodiles	31
The Maiden of Unai	35
The Story of the man who did not wish to die	39
The Happy Hunter and the Skillful Fisher	44
The Tale of the Bamboo Cutter	51
The Crab and the Monkey	60
Mandarin Ducks	62
The Old Woman who lost her Dumpling.	64
The Spring Lover and the Autumn Lover	68
The Flute	71
The Boy who drew Cats	74
The Wooden Bowl	77
Reflections	80
The Good Thunder	86
A Legend of Kwannon	90
The Goblin of Adachigahara	93
About the Author	**96**

Preface

This book emphasizes the importance of education as every great dream begins with the dreamer. The intrinsic motivation to learn about the world begins in infancy. The ingredients of play stress on the curiosity aspect of children and the exposure to surroundings. A book takes you to the right places where you have fun while you learn. The strangest gift in the world is a book which contains tales of gathering describing our culture and traditions, something like a mirror which gives you back yourself.

Here there are wild things which become our friends. A kind of story which is passed down from generation to generation. When people belonged to a tribe or lived in villages by necessity or by creation there emerged a variety of ideas which led to conflict and needed to be stabilized. A folk tale includes characters good or evil, hero and heroine, magic and mayhem. It is often pictured as beginning with "Once upon a time" and resolved through kindness, courage and intelligence.

Folktales were made up to explain the wonders of life and teach moral values and lessons usually through a character and in the end good is rewarded and evil is punished but it is a fact that all tales have a happy ending.

Folklore is oral history preserved by the people to provide information regarding the origin of a group of people who belong to a specific place and follow the same culture. We as unique individuals are connected through these moral truths. They give us wisdom to observe things from different points of view.

The five types of Folktales include fairy tales, legends, myths, tall tales and fables. It has the power to influence or change a person. The stories are of a particular place adhering to justice, rights and social obligations of its citizens.

Introduction

Japan is popularly known as the "Land of the Rising Sun" and in Japanese, Japan is called 'Nippon' which means 'source of the sun'.

Japanese folktales claim it's influence from various sources.

Japan is known for its beautiful landscapes, ancient temples and shrines and its vibrant cities, delicious cuisine, art, fashion and nightlife.

Japanese people always display modesty and bow to convey the message: "I am not above you. I respect you." This is part of their tradition. Consideration and thoughtfulness permeate every aspect of life in Japan. The most recognizable symbol of Japanese art is Cherry Blossom which is widely used in poetry.

The three main religions of Japan are Shinto, Buddhism and Confucianism. The official language is Japanese spoken by a vast majority of the population. Folktales of Japan have been handed down from generations by word of mouth and they distinctly fit between the idea of a folktale and folklore, the imposters being the tales which are written literary pieces dating back to the Muromachi period or the Middle Ages. The first systematic collection of specimens was pioneered by Kunio Yanagita who stated that the actual old folk he had collected were different from the term folktales which went along with the conventions of other countries and used the term mukashibanashi or tales of long ago to apply to creative type of folktales. Such stories often featured figures like the kani, or spirits, and Oni or demons. Two very common tales known in Japan are of Momotaro, the boy born from a peach and the tongue-cut sparrow which appear in this book.

What makes Japan unique are its architecture, art, traditions, crafts and pop culture including manga, anime and video games which is definitely what only Japan can offer. Japan is famous for its rich cultural history and unique blend of modern and traditional culture.

The Two Frogs

Once upon a time in the country of Japan there lived two frogs. One Frog lived in a ditch near the town of Osaka on the sea coast. The other frog lived in a clear little stream that ran through the city of Kyoto.

The Two Frogs is a story of Two amphibians who live in different cities in Japan. In Japan frogs are a symbol of good luck. Frogs are seen as iconic creatures who are a sign of good fortune. The word "frog" in Japanese means "to return" and frogs are linked to things or people returning to their place of origin.

They are believed to possess magical powers and bring long life and money to people around them. Tago's brown frog is a species found commonly in Japan. It is a remarkable expression of the natural environment of Japan.

The Kaeru shrine, the god of which is a Frog, is worshiped in Japan. The origin of this tradition came because frogs are found near water which is essential to survive. The presence of frogs indicates lifesaving water. These creatures are used in poetry or art and are linked to the cycle of nature and life. According to legends frogs can breathe out rainbows to slide prey into their mouths.

This is the story of two frogs from Japan. They lived apart from one another in two different cities and had never seen or heard of each other. One day a thought struck them, they got two ideas at the same exact moment. The frogs wanted to see the new world. They were very much desirous of seeing the outside world and held their own opinions about the world outside their realms.

The frogs did not know each other but interestingly had the same grit to explore the new world outside them. The frog who lived in Kyoto wanted to visit Osaka and the frog which lived in Osaka wanted to visit Kyoto. The frog who lived in the swamp at Osaka wanted to see the glorious palace of Mikado which was termed the most beautiful in Kyoto. It wanted to experience for itself the beauty of Kyoto.

Funnily at the same time the Frog who lived in the crystal-clear waters of Kyoto was judging its own home and was quite proud of the place. The frog understood that the palace of Mikado was indeed a fine place and had nothing personal against the emperor of the country. But it wanted to go to Osaka vary of the beauty around. The frog had decided to experience something more subtle, bored of the beauty which always existed in the place of Kyoto.

Know that a tall mountain separated Kyoto from Osaka. Both frogs jumped out of their place to set out on an adventure. The frog from Osaka made efforts to climb over and above the mountain while the frog from Kyoto drenched out his whole strength to reach Osaka. They were both excited to see the brand-new world. So, one fine morning they embarked on this journey but carried little or no knowledge about traveling. It took them many hops and pings to reach the top.

The journey was very tiring and distraught. It was more of a challenge than they had expected. It took them a long time to reach the top of the mountain and the result was very unexpected. They were surprised to see each other. Just imagine another fellow frog standing in front at the crossroads of the journey!

The frogs looked at each other for a moment so afraid of losing sight of each other. They stared at each other not believing what their eyes gave them. Our very own eyes give us the truth that is so unsustainable yet absorbing at the same time.

They immediately began talking and chatting like the whole world falling right into their laps. It was so unnerving that they both had the same desire. But astoundingly neither was in a hurry to gather the other. Neither frog was worried and their eyes bulged with delight as they carried on the conversation.

They both squatted to catch their breaths and rest their legs considering themselves as the great explorers of the entire world.

At last everything felt in place as they introduced themselves. The frog from Kyoto retold the beauty at his place which he thought was unbearable. The land of palaces seemed to him touching. The frog from Osaka who was from the swamp greeted the other frog with a loud croak and declared that Osaka was a miserable place. It thought that the place where a frog really could enjoy was Kyoto where there existed a crystal-clear stream of water.

The frog from Kyoto let his heart out described the beauty of the lake to be so sparkling that out of regret it was nothing but sparkle that gave frogs to gather what is called happiness.

Suddenly the frogs fell silent as they stared at each other. The frog from Kyoto decided that the frog from Osaka was not very much different from itself in shape, structure and size. And the frog from Osaka was relieved that the frog from Kyoto was an exact replica.

The frogs, now submissive of their homes, went on to play the game of looking into each other's eyes as if they had no other intention but so much filled with little indifference. And so, the two frogs exchanged their thoughts. The frog from Kyoto understood that climbing the mountain was tiring to descend to Osaka since the place was relatively dull as the other frog made out in the conversation. The frog from Osaka felt the same way and declared that the sparkling stream may not be as beautiful as expected and it was too tired to hop all the way.

Again, they sat in silence now maybe waiting for another pedestrian like them who would give them a difference of opinion. They both sighed deeply and again stared at each other, dubious of themselves. It was unworthy to continue this journey in their intellectual minds so longing to measure the world with just their eyes. They, of their high capacity of intellectual integrity, came upon an idea.

The grass was tall. If they held onto each other by their hind legs for balance and stretched themselves as high as possible they could see the other side and take in the view of the city they hoped to reach. The Kyoto frog turned its nose towards Osaka and the Osaka frog turned its nose towards Kyoto. But the frogs were silly. With their nose pointing to the towns that they wanted their eyes pointed back to the towns where they came from. It was a stupid idea.

The Frog from Osaka received the idea that Kyoto was exactly like Osaka and the Frog from Kyoto decided that the place of Osaka was a copy of Kyoto.

They, at the engaged beauty of what their eyes saw, fell down on to the grass exhausted and lost their balance. They had enough of the beauty which was so dearly alike. But both of them were sad since the places were similar and so disengaged that they had wasted their time.

At last, both exchanged their goodbyes and set off for their homes believing to the end of their lives that the place they hoped to see was as good as any other home and almost the same like two peas in a pod.

The Tongue-Cut Sparrow

Once upon a time there was an old man who lived all alone. There was an old woman who lived all alone. The old man was kind and hardworking. The old woman was greedy and mean. They had no children. As they grew older, they had to work even harder to survive. The old man found a pet. It was a little sparrow. He nurtured the sparrow as his own child and taught it many kinds of tricks. The sparrow soon became the apple of his eyes. It was very good company and when the old man came back from work each night there would be the sparrow twittering on the doorstep "Welcome home master." The sparrow's sweet singing brought happiness into the old man's life. But his wife did not like the sparrow and considered it a silly bird.

One day the old man went away to cut wood. She had made some good starch which she had laid out in a wooden bowl since it was her day of washing clothes. The little sparrow flew over the bamboo fence and lighted on the edge of a starch bowl while her back was turned and pecked at some of the starch. The sparrow made a good meal out of it. The old woman was very mad at the sparrow and flew into a rage. With a pair of scissors, she cut off the tongue of the sparrow. The poor bird flew away to the woods.

The old man came from the hills and found that the bird had flown away. He enquired about the sparrow and what had become of it. The old woman answered that she had cut the tongue of the sparrow and let it go. The next morning the old man went to the woods to find the little sparrow. Everywhere he went he cried, "Where are you little sparrow, my friend?"

The woods grew thick and dark and the old man was worried that he could never see the sparrow again. Over the mountains and Dale, the old man searched for the sparrow without hope. "Sparrow, Sparrow, where are you, my tongue cut sparrow?" was all he spoke. With great sadness he called out to the sparrow to come home. "Little sparrow, please come home," the old man said repeatedly.

He wandered far and wide for his pet crying:

"Mr. Sparrow! Mr. Sparrow! Where are you living?"

At last, he came across the house of the sparrow. The sparrow flew out to greet his master. And to his great surprise he heard the sparrow speak.

"Old man, you have been very kind to me. It is time for me to return the kindness". She led the old man to a little house with a bamboo garden and a tiny waterfall. "Come and meet my family," said the Sparrow. The Sparrow called his brothers and sisters and his children and his wife. And he also called out to his mother-in-law and his mother and his grandmother. They all flew to honor the old man. The old man removed his shoes and entered the house. They set him down on mats of silk. They served the old man a delicious meal. It consisted of rice cakes, sweet candies and hot tea. Then they did a dance which brought joy to his heart. The Sparrow waited on the old man with his brothers and sisters and his wife and his children and his mother-in-law and his mother and his grandmother with him. It was a merry evening.

"What a polite and lovely Sparrow!" the old man remarked. The old man stayed as a guest of the Sparrow for a very long time. He was daily treated royally. At last, the old man said that he must take leave and return home. "Before you go, please accept a little gift," said the sparrow. She placed two baskets in front of the old man. One was big and heavy. The other was small and light. The Sparrow instructed the old man to choose one of the baskets and asked him not to open the basket until he reached home.

The old man would rather have the sparrow than any other present but the sparrow refused to go with the old man. The old man was not greedy and chose the small basket. "It would suit me to carry the light basket," said the old man. As I am not as young as I once was." With many thanks the old man returned home.

So he went home with the light basket and told his wife all that had happened. When he opened it, the basket was full of gold and silver and tortoise shell and coral and jade and fine rolls of silk. The old man was delighted. But his wife was angry as the old man had not brought home the big basket which was heavy. Without a word she hurried into the woods to find the Sparrow's home.

Over hill and over dale she went to find the house of the Sparrow. There was the Sparrow with his brothers and his sisters and his wife and children and his mother-in-law and his mother and his grandmother. They were not too pleased to see the old bad woman.

However, the polite Sparrow invited her into the house and served some hot tea. She took one sip and had enough of the tea. She remarked that it was late and she had to return home. She wanted to leave immediately. As estimated by the old woman, the Sparrow brought out two baskets. One was big and one was small. The Sparrow urged the woman to choose one basket and not to open the basket until she returned home. The old woman grabbed the big basket but, on the way, sat down to rest. She did not want to wait. She wanted to get a peek inside the heavy basket.

Instead of gold and silver it was filled with toads that leaped on her and got into her belongings. She was very afraid of frogs and cried out loud. Snakes slithered on her arms and legs and wasps stung her and pricked her skin. The old woman screamed and ran as fast as she could. The old woman got better after a few days and regretted her mistake. She thought that it was not right on her part to be too greedy and that she should not have hurt the sparrow.

They adopted a son and the old man soon grew rich and prosperous. And they lived happily ever after.

The Stonecutter

Once there was a poor stonecutter. Each day he went to the mountain and cut blocks of stone. He then took them to the market to sell them. He understood very well the different kinds of stones wanted by his customers as he was a very careful workman. For a long time, he was quite happy. He wanted nothing better than the work he had. He was very happy until he looked through the gates of a rich man. He saw the rich man sitting under the shade of a banyan tree and eating rich food brought by the servants.

He thought to himself, "Surely the rich man must be very happy!"

I think he is greater than I am.

Soon he wanted to lead his life like the rich man with good food to eat.

"If only I were rich" he reflected." I would be a happier man."

The spirit of the mountain was flying around and heard the stonecutter. It gave him all that the stonecutter wanted. At once the stonecutter found himself sitting under the same tree in the same garden being served with rich food by a number of servants.

He was truly happy. But after a while he did not feel inclined to do his work.

But when he reached the little house where he lived, he stood still with amazement, for instead of his hut there was a stately palace filled with furniture and a splendid bed like the one he had perceived. He was beside himself with joy. He soon forgot his old life.

It was now the beginning of summer and as the sun blazed fiercely the stonecutter found it difficult to work. He peeped outside his window onto the streets and felt for the luxurious palace of the king himself. There he saw more servants bringing food and serving the king. And understood the ridiculously splendid lifestyle of the king. He wanted to be like the king who led a happier life. "Surely, the king is greater;" thought the stonecutter." If only I were the King, I would be truly happy!" No more heavy lifting, No more slabs of rock.

The spirit of the mountain heard the stonecutter and again gave him what he wanted. But after a few days when he was standing outside and the sun was beating down on his head, he felt very hot and urged himself to go inside and relax thus leaving his work incomplete. The sun was very annoying. It scorched the earth and burned the back of the emperor.

"Surely, the sun is greater than I am!" He wanted to be like the sun which was the greatest entity that was complimenting every aspect of his life. He wished and he wished and then the magic happened. All of a sudden, the stonecutter got what he wanted. Though his life as an emperor was pretty fantastic, he got to thinking, what would it like to be the sun?

Before he knew it, the emperor became the sun!. And life was fabulous. It was great to float all day in the sky, shining down upon the earth and the life on it. As the sun he could order the process of photosynthesis by which plants made their food. And could scorch the people and force them to stay home. And damage the crops and make the farmers cry. Give the women a little sunburn and force the children to remove clothes or make them scream and act weird. This was interesting and madly comforting. The stonecutter felt beautiful.

One day something strange happened when he was floating around his own village. His rays were being blocked by something. There were big shadows appearing under him. The rays of the sun could not get through even as the stonecutter puffed more and more. It was however useless since a cloud had come between the sun and the village. This cloud was blocking the sun so that no one could see him. Why was this happening? He hopped and hoped and wished and wished to be greater....

Then the magic happened. The sun became a cloud.

"Surely, the cloud is greater than I am!" thought the sun. "If only I was the cloud, then I would be truly happy."

The spirit of the mountain heard the sun and gave him what he wanted. At once the stonecutter became a cloud. As a cloud he could block the rays of the sun. He could shapeshift into all kinds of things of different shapes and sizes much to the amusement of the village children. And perhaps he could make it rain. This was a lot of fun. And it rained and rained and rained.

The cloud loved the plants. He felt that giving life was important. Life surely could not survive without water. He could also let down thunder and bolts. Lire as a cloud was truly amazing.

But one day as the cloud was drifting above his village the wind took the cloud in a different direction. Why could he not float where he wished? Who was interfering with his beautiful life? The cloud got thinking and thinking….

So, he wished and wished and then the magic happened….

Soon enough the cloud became the wind. And life was even better.! It was fun to push the clouds and make leaves blow off trees and hair stand on end and make goosebumps on the arms of people. And send tornadoes across the earth or create cyclones of destruction. This certainly was fun.

One day the wind crashed through the air into something hard. It tried to push the thing but without luck and went around in circles but the structure was too massive to break through. This was not fun. Something was blocking his path. It was a mountain. So, the wind got to thinking and wished and wished and wished…..

Again, the magic happened. That is the wind turned into a mountain. The stonecutter became strong and firm.

But one day as the mountain was relaxing and reflecting on his life he felt something pricking. What was happening?

Being a mountain was supposed to be perfect. Ouch!

He noticed a stonecutter crossing the mountain as he cut blocks of stones from the mountains and took it away. And the mountain wished and wished…..

"Surely the stone cutter is greater than I am," he sighed. "If only I was a stonecutter".

To his astonishment the mountain became the stonecutter once again. He was back to his initial life of cutting stones and breaking slabs of rock and taking them down to the village. From that day the stonecutter never wished again.

He was thankful and never wished again to be something he was not. There could not be any life better or satisfying like that of the stonecutter. Though there were days he worked under the blazing sun, the wet rain, the chilly wind, he never complained. He was content with his life as a stonecutter.

The Mirror of Matsuyama

Once upon a time in the province of Echigo in a very remote part of Japan lived a man and his wife. They had a daughter whom they loved very much. She was beautiful.

One day the father had to go to Kyoto for business. The father promised to bring a gift to the daughter if she behaved well and listened to her mother when he was gone. He then departed for his journey. The mother was a little frightened, for she has never ventured further than her village. The very thought of her husband taking a long journey was scary. Even Though this was true the woman was proud of her husband. He was the first person from the countryside to embark on such a long journey to the town. The town was the place of the King and where the Great Lords resided. And in the town, there were many beautiful and curious things of interest to the mind.

At last, the time came when the man had to return. The woman dressed the girl in her best clothes. And on herself she put on a pretty blue dress which she knew her husband liked.

The father returned after a month. His wife and daughter welcomed him. He took forever his hat and sandals and sat on the floor. The little girl clapped her hands with joy and the woman was very glad to see him come home safe. Then he opened his bamboo basket. The daughter laughed in delight at the pretty toys her father had brought home. He had much to talk about the wonderful things he had seen in the town.

As the daughter eagerly watched, the father took out a beautiful doll and a lacquer box of cakes from the basket. Once more he dived into the basket and presented his wife with a metal mirror. The surface of the mirror shined brightly. On the back of the mirror there was a design of pine trees and storks.

The wife had never seen a mirror before. The wife was amazed to see such a mirror. The man remarked, "Look and tell me what you can see inside." When she gazed into the mirror she was filled with wonder. From the depths was looking at her with parted lips and bright eyes, a happy face. The man explained about the mirror and the woman added it amongst her treasures. The man was glad to show that he had learned something while he had been away.

He exclaimed, "That round piece of metal is called a mirror."

In town everyone has one of these. The wife was charmed by the mirror and didn't use it often. It was the first time she had seen the reflection of her own pretty face. She considered such a wonderful thing too precious for everyday use.

Years passed and the family lived very happily. The joy of their life was the daughter who had grown to be the replica of her mother. She was dutiful and affectionate and everybody loved her. She was simple and knew nothing about her good looks or the mirror.

The mother never spoke of the mirror and the father had forgotten about it. Mindful of her own good looks she kept the mirror carefully hidden fearing that the use of it might breed a spirit of pride in her little girl.

After a few years the living mother fell sick. The daughter waited upon her mother day and night but to no effect. The mother got so worse that there was no doubt that she would die. The poor woman grieved for the family she was going to leave behind.

The mother called her daughter and declared that she was sick and would soon die. She urged her daughter to take good care of her father. She presented the daughter with the mirror. When the mother was gone and the daughter felt lonely, she would look into the mirror and feel happy thus assuring the girl of her presence and supervision. The mother died a short while later.

"When you feel lonely, look into it and you will always see me smiling at you."

In due time the man married again. And the obedient daughter never forgot the last request of her mother. She had hidden the mirror and everyday would find the bright smiling face of her mother in the mirror. To the mirror during the night, she would tell tales of her difficulties and during the day find inspiration and sympathy in the same. Her greatest joy was the mirror.

The stepmother was not kind to her daughter. The daughter remembering the words of her mother would sit in a corner and look into the mirror. Seeing her look into the mirror day and night without fail and converse at length with it frightened the stepmother. The stepmother, herself ignorant of the thing called a mirror, complained to the father of his daughter using witchcraft against her.

The father was furious to hear this. The father asked her the reason for her strange behavior. The daughter explained to her father that it was the dying wish of her mother.

"Father" she said, "I look in the mirror every day to talk to my dear mother."

Touched by the simplicity and the faithful, loving obedience of his child the father shed tears of pity and affection.

All misunderstandings were cleared. The father began to love his daughter even more. The stepmother heard their conversations and felt ashamed. She apologized for her behavior and asked the girl for forgiveness. The girl willingly forgave her stepmother and never bore any malice towards her. They all lived happily ever after.

The daughter still cherished the memory of her real mother. Both the father and stepmother were touched by the daughter's love for her mother.

In Japan there is a tradition of respecting Parents. This story is an example of what it is to be a good daughter.

The Adventures of Little Peachling

Once upon a time there lived an honest woodcutter and his wife. One fine morning the old man went to the forest to collect wood and his wife went to the river to wash the dirty clothes. When she came down to the river she saw a peach floating. She picked it up and carried it home with her. She wanted to give it to her husband to eat. She then quickly finished her washing and returned home.

When she took it up and looked at it she saw that it was a very large peach. When she cut the peach in two out came a child from the kernel. Seeing this the joy of the couple knew no bounds. They named the child Momotaro or Little Peachling because the child had come out of a peach.

The couple took good care of Little Peachling who grew up to be a strong boy. The couple had high expectations regarding Little Peachling and bestowed him with the finest education. He was a very brave boy and decided to go to a neighboring island of ogres and devils to bring back riches for his parents.

He asked the old woman to make him some dumplings for the journey. The old woman gave him a sack of dumplings. Little Peachling after taking an affectionate leave of them cheerfully set on his journey.

On his journey to the island a monkey approached the boy. It asked, "Where are you going, Little Peachling?"

Peachling answered that he was going to the ogres island to carry treasure to his parents.

"What are you carrying in your girdle?"; enquired the monkey.

"I am Carrying the very best millet dumplings in the whole of Japan."

"If you give me one, I will go with you."

So, Little Peachling gave one of his dumplings to the monkey who received it and followed him.

When they had gone a little further, he heard a Pheasant calling: "Ken! Ken! Ken!, where are you going, Master Peachling?"

Little Peachling answered as before. The Pheasant, having begged and obtained a millet dumpling, entered his service and followed him.

A little while later they met a dog who cried: "Bow! WoW! WoW! wither away, Master Peachling?"

"I am going to the ogres island to carry off treasure"

"If you give me one of those millet dumplings of yours, I will go with you," said the dog.

Little Peachling agreed. So, he went on his way with the

Monkey, Pheasant and the dog followed after him.

When they came to the castle, the Pheasant flew over the gate, the monkey clambered over the castle wall and the Little Peachling forced his entry into the gate with the dog and entered the castle. Then they did battle with the ogres who took to flight and they took the King prisoner.

All the ogres paid homage to Little Peachling. They brought out all their treasures and laid it before them. There were clothes and hats that made the wearer invisible. There were jewels which were exquisite and coral, musk, emeralds, tortoise shells besides silver and gold. All these mind-boggling treasures were laid in front of Little Peachling and company.

Little Peachling went home with the treasure. He lived with his foster parents in peace and plenty. They lived in pomp and glory happily ever after.

My Lord Bag of Rice

Once upon a time there lived a brave warrior in Japan by the name Tawara Toda or 'My Lord Bag of Rice.' His real name was Fujiwara Hidesato. The story of how he derived his nickname is an exciting tale of courage, commitment and adventure.

One day he set off in search of an adventure, carrying two swords, a huge bow and a quiver full of arrows for he could not bear to be idle. He had not gone far when he came to the bridge of Seta-no-Karashi spanning the beautiful Lake Biwa. No sooner had he set foot on the bridge he came across a huge serpent-dragon spanning the lake.

It had a big body which looked like the trunk of a large pine tree and took up the whole width of the bridge. One of his claws rested on the parapet of one side of the bridge while the tail lay right against the other. The monster seemed to be asleep.

It breathed fire and smoke came out of its nostrils. Hidesato at first felt alarmed at the sight of the horrible reptile. He had no choice other than walk over it or turn back. But Hidesato was a very brave man who put aside his fear and felt determined to walk across the bridge. Without a glance he went in his way without turning his back.

Crunch! Crunch! He stepped on the body of the Dragon. He had only gone a few steps when he heard someone calling his name from behind. On turning back, he noticed that the Monster had disappeared. In its place was a weird looking man who was ceremoniously bowing to the ground. His red hair was steaming down his shoulders and was surmounted by a crown in the shape of a dragon's head and his sea-green dress was patterned with shells.

At once Hidesato understood that this was no ordinary mortal. He wondered about the dragon. Where had the dragon gone? What did the whole thing mean? Was this man the dragon in disguise? While these thoughts passed through his mind he came to the strange man. Fujiwara addressed the man "Was it you that called me just now?"

The man answered with a nod and replied "Yes." I have an earnest request to make to you. Do you think you can grant it to me?

"I am the Dragon King of this lake. There comes a wicked centipede every night to take away one of my family."

"I have waited a long time for a brave warrior to save my several children and grandchildren. You are the first man who was brave enough to cross over the bridge."

For many days with this intention, I have waited on the bridge in the shape of the horrible serpent-dragon that you saw in hope that a strong man would come along the way. I beg you to have pity upon me.

"Will you kill the centipede?"

Hidesato felt very sorry for the Dragon King on hearing his story. Hidesato agreed and the Dragon King took him to his Palace near the lake. As he followed his host the waters of the lake parted to make way. Never had Hidesato seen something as beautiful as the Palace. It was built of white marble. He had often heard of the Palace of the Sea-King at the bottom of the sea. There he was welcomed and looked after with great love and honor. The dainty gold fishes, red carp and silver trout waited upon the dragon king and his guest.

The centipede lived on the mountain Mikami and came out every night at a certain hour to the palace of the lake.

Hidesato was astonished at the feast spread in his name. The dishes were crystallized lotus leaves and flowers, and the chopsticks were of the rarest ebony. As soon as they sat down the sliding doors opened and ten lovely dancers came out and behind them followed ten red carp musicians with the koto and the harp. The hours flew by till midnight and the beautiful music banished all thoughts of the centipede.

Then after a while when the host was about to pledge a second cup of wine to Fujiwara the palace was shaken suddenly as if a mighty army was marching inside. Hidesato and the Dragon King both rose to their feet and rushed to the balcony. In the dark he could see two glowing orbs of light which were the eyes of the creature. He aimed his bow and fired an arrow towards the centipede. It fell without causing harm to the creature. The same thing happened with the second arrow.

Hidesato now had only one arrow remaining.

He remembered that he had once heard that human saliva was poisonous to centipedes and so he placed the next arrow in his mouth before sending it flying towards the monster. This time the arrow went and struck the brain. The creature began to shudder and shake. There were crashes of thunder as the enormous centipede fell to its death, flailing his hundred legs. As the first light of dawn appeared Hidesato called out to the Dragon King and advised them that the centipede was dead.

At last, the dreadful night was over and the centipede was gone from the mountain.

The gratitude of the king knew no bounds. The whole family came and bowed down before the warrior calling him the bravest warrior in all Japan.

The Dragon-King was so delighted at being free that another feast was held to honor Hidesato to express gratitude. All kinds of fish prepared in every imaginable way raw, stewed, boiled and roasted were served on coral trays and crystal dishes. The wine was the best Hidesato had ever tasted. He was seen off with rich gifts and some special gifts. A bell, a bag of rice, a roll of silk and a cooking pot.

His host tried to persuade the warrior to stay a few days but Hidesato insisted on going home. He had finished what he had come to do and must return. The Dragon-King and family were all sorry to have him leave so soon.

As the warrior stood in the porch taking leave, a train of fish was transformed into a retinue of men all wearing ceremonial robes and crown in the shape of a dragon on their heads indicating that they were slaves of the King.

The dragon accompanied Hidesato till the bridge.

Hidesato did not want to accept the presents but also he could not refuse the Dragon King. Hidesato returned to his Palace. The presents he had got seemed to contain magical powers. The bell was put up to mark the hours. It was presented to the temple nearby where it was hung up to boom out the hour of the day over the surrounding neighborhood. The rice bag was never empty. It was used day after day for the meals of the knights and the family. The Cooking Pot would cook anything that was put into it and the roll of silk never finished. Long pieces were cut off to make the warrior a new suit of clothes to go to the court on the New Year.

The fame of Hidesato spread far and wide. There was no need for him to spend money on rice or silk. He became very rich and prosperous. And was henceforth known as "My Lord Bag of Rice."

The Farmer and the Badger

Once upon a time there lived an old farmer with his wife. They lived on the mountains and had no neighbors except for the badger. The badger would always come and ruin the farmers' plants and mess up the house. It would run across the field and would spoil the vegetables patches and the rice he grew. The badger at last grew so ruthless that the farmer could not stand it anymore and was determined to put a stop to this.

So, he lay in wait day after day and night after night for the badger with a big club hoping to catch the badger. He even laid traps to catch the badger. But not all were in vain as the farmers' efforts were soon rewarded. One fine day when he was going on his morning rounds, he found the badger caught in a hole. The farmer was delighted. He carried the badger home securely bound by a rope.

"I have at last caught the badger," replied the farmer." Make sure that this badger does not escape." They readily agreed to each other to make soup out of the badger. The badger was tied upside down and fastened to the ceiling as the farmer left for the fields and the wife too went about her work.

Meanwhile the badger was making plans for his escape. He thought about it and looked at the lady making a soulful face. It was hard to think clearly in his uncomfortable position.

At the entrance of the house looking towards the fields in the pleasant sunshine stood the farmer's wife who was pounding barley. She looked tired and exhausted. Every now and then she stopped to wipe the sweat off her face.

The wily badger observing this formed a good plan of escape. He confronted the lady, "Would you let me do the work for you?"

"I have strong arms," persuaded the badger.

The woman thanked the badger for his kindness and retorted, "You will escape if I untie you."

She went on, "My husband will be very angry if I let you go."

Now, the badger was the most cunning of animals. It replied, "If you are afraid of your husband, I will let you bind me again after the work is done."

The woman was kind and simple. She could not think badly of any person. She did not think that the badger would deceive her. She felt sorry for the animal. She fell in love with the innocent face. The woman released the badger. The badger at once sprang on the woman and knocked her down with a heavy piece of wood. He killed her and made soup out of her.

The old man there with the thought of his fields being safe and of the pleasure that his labor would not go undone left for his home. The badger had assumed the form of the old woman. It came out to greet the old man on the verandah of the little house.

The old man took off his sandals and sat down before his dinner tray. The innocent man had never dreamed that it was not his wife that was waiting upon him and asked at once for the soup. The badger suddenly transformed himself back to his natural form.

It cried, "Look out for the bones of the old woman."

"Your wife was devoured by me," laughed the badger and ran away to his den on the hills.

The old man was left all alone. He cried loudly and bitterly and rocked himself hopelessly. It seemed so surreal that his faithful wife was made into soup. The farmer who had been congratulating himself for the deed of trapping the badger felt grieved with strife. He had nearly drunk the soup made from the blood and flesh of his own wife. He wailed, "Oh! dear, dear!"

Now not far away there in the nearby mountain lived a rabbit. He heard the old man crying and sobbing. The rabbit decided to visit the old man to enquire about the happenings. The old man told him all that had happened. The rabbit was at once horrified about what the deceitful badger had done. It at once resolved to avenge the death of the old woman. The farmer was at last comforted. He thanked the rabbit for his goodness in coming to his aid.

The next day the weather was fine and the rabbit went out to find the badger. The badger was not to be seen in the woods. So the rabbit decided to go to the den and found the badger hiding there itself for fear of the wrath of the old man.

The rabbit called out to the badger; "What are you doing inside on such a beautiful day?"

"Please come outside and we will go and cut the grass on the hills together."

The badger didn't doubt the rabbit at all for the cordial remark. He accepted the rabbit as his friend and consented to go out with the rabbit. They both set to work. They cut down as much grass as possible to store up for the winter, tied it in bundles and made their way homewards.

On the way home, the rabbit took out a flint and struck the bundle of grass on the back of the badger, setting the bundle of grass on fire. The badger asked the rabbit, "What is that noise?"

"That is nothing," replied the rabbit. The fire soon spread and the back of the badger caught fire.

The badger hearing the crackle again asked, "What is that?"

"We have come to the burning mountain," consoled the rabbit.

There was the smell of the smoke of the burning grass. The badger screamed with pain and ran to his hole. The rabbit followed and found the badger lying on his bed groaning with pain. The punishment of the badger had just begun. All the hair on the badger's back was burnt. The badger did not feel even remotely bad for the badger as it was guilty of killing the poor old woman. He went home and made an ointment mixing some sauce and red pepper together.

The rabbit applied the ointment on the badger. The badger should bear the pain for it was a good medicine against the burns. No language could describe the agony the badger felt at that time. The badger rolled over and over and howled loudly.

The rabbit felt that the farmer's wife was being avenged. The badger was in the bed for a month. In Spite of the ointment the wounds of the badger had healed. The rabbit thought of another plan. The rabbit visited the badger and congratulated him on the recovery.

During the conversation the badger mentioned that he was going fishing. The rabbit described how pleasant the activity of fishing was and how it soothes the soul. The badger listened with pleasure to this account. He asked the rabbit if he would take the badger along, the next time he went fishing to which the rabbit readily agreed.

The rabbit went home and built two boats. One was of wood and the other was of clay. At last, they were finished. The rabbit looked at his work and felt that his prayers would soon be answered. If the plan succeeded the badger would soon meet his doom.

The day soon came and the rabbit kept the wooden boat for himself. The badger who knew nothing about boats was delighted about fishing in the new boat and thought that the rabbit was being very kind. They both got into their boats and set out. The rabbit challenged the badger in a race to which the latter readily accepted. They both began to row as fast as they could. In the middle of the race the badger found his boat crumbling into pieces. He cried out in great fear and asked the rabbit to help him out. The badger who was avenging the murder of the old woman refused. It was happy to think that the badger would meet his end. The badger was drowning with nobody to help him out. It raised the oars and struck the badger on its head. The badger soon sank and was not to be seen.

The rabbit has kept his promise to the old man. The badger turned back homewards to report to the old man on how the badger had been killed.

The old man thanked the rabbit with tears in his eyes. The old man could sleep at night and be at peace in the morning. The death of his wife was finally avenged. He begged the rabbit to stay with him. From that day the rabbit began to stay with the old farmer. They both lived together as good friends for years to come to the end of his days.

The Jellyfish and the Monkey

Long ago in old Japan there lived a wonderful king who was very powerful for he ruled over all sea creatures big and small. His name was Ryn Jin and in his keeping were the Jewels of the Ebb and Flow of the tide. The Jewel of the Ebbing tide when thrown into the ocean caused the water to recede and the Jewel of the flowing tide made the waves rise high above to the level of a mountain.

The Palace of Ryn Jin was the most beautiful thing that a living person could ever see in this world. The walls were of coral, the roof made of jade and the floors were made of pearls. But the Dragon King, in spite of all this wealth, was not happy. He was not married and had no children. At last, the king decided to marry and take a wife. For a long time, the King and Queen lived very happily but their joy was short lived. Soon, the Queen fell very ill and was on her deathbed.

The swiftest messengers were sent to fetch the best doctors from every country but it was of no use. Everyone had given up hope when one day a doctor arrived who was cleverer than the rest. The only thing that could cure her was the liver of a monkey.

"Heart's Desire," he said to his pale bride, "I would give my life for you."

She answered," If you fetch me a monkey's liver, I will eat it and live."

"If I do not have the liver, I shall die"

Then the doctor told the King that some distance to the south there was a Monkey Island where many monkeys lived. The monkeys lived on dry land while they lived on water.

The king called his chief steward and others and consulted on the matter. The steward thought for some time and an idea suddenly struck him.

There was a huge Jellyfish who was ugly to look at but was proud of being able to walk on land with his four legs like a tortoise. They made the idea to send the Jellyfish to the land of monkeys to catch one.

"Now go and fetch me a monkey, O jellyfish as I have heard that they live on the tall trees of the forest on Monkey Island."

"How will I get the monkey to come back with me?" said the Jellyfish

"Tell him of the beauty of the ocean and of his happy life with the mermaids"

"You must carry the monkey on your back. What is the use of your shell if you can't do that!"

Off set the Jellyfish and swam and swam till he reached the shore. He saw a monkey playing near the seashore. On looking around he saw a big pine tree where a live monkey was sitting on the dropping branches.

Children must often have wondered why jelly-fishes have no shells. In old times this was not so; the jellyfish had as hard a shell as any one of the creatures that are washed up daily on the beach. But it lost the shell through its own fault.

The Jellyfish raised his voice "How do you do, Mr Monkey?"

"A very fine day," answered the monkey.

"I have not seen you in this part of the world."

"Where have you come from and what is your name?"

"My name is Kurage or jellyfish."

"I am one of the servants of the Dragon King"

"By the way have you seen the Palace of the king where I come from?" asked the Jellyfish.

"The beauty of the Palace is beyond all descriptions"

"Is it as beautiful as all that?" retorted the monkey

The Jellyfish saw his chance and went on describing the beauty of the Palace. The wonders of the garden with its curious trees of white, pink and red coral and the still more curious fruits like great jewels hanging from the branches.

The monkey grew more and more interested.

"I should love to go," said the monkey.

"There is no difficulty. I can carry you on my back"

"I am stronger than you think and need not hesitate."

And taking the monkey on his back it stepped into the sea.

"Keep very still Mr Monkey. I am responsible for your safety," said the Jellyfish.

"Please don't go fast, or I am sure I shall fall off," said the monkey.

Thus they went along with the Jellyfish skimming through the waves with the monkey on his back. As they reached halfway the Jellyfish who knew very little about anatomy began to get worried. It began to wonder whether the monkey had a liver with him or not!

"Mr Monkey, tell me, do you have such a thing as a liver with you?"

The monkey was surprised at this queer question. The monkey grew more and more suspicious and ended up saying that it was troubled and worried about what he had been told.

The Jellyfish felt sorry for the monkey and told him everything. How the Dragon Queen had fallen ill and how only the liver of a monkey could cure the Queen.

And also explained that it had done what was required of the Jellyfish.

The poor monkey was horrified at the story and felt it wise not to administer the fear it felt. He tried to calm himself and think of some way by which he might escape.

The monkey said that he had forgotten his liver hanging on a tree. He had hung it to dry in the sun. If it rained it would get wet. So, he wanted to go back to the tree to get his liver.

The Jellyfish carried him back to the seashore. Back they went and the monkey was up in the persimmon tree in a twinkling.

"Mercy me, where can I have mislaid it?"

"I should not be surprised if some rascal has stolen it."

Now the Jellyfish had no schooling and its grandmother always said that the jellyfish would come to a bad end.

"I shall take some time finding the liver. You should not be out in the dark. Sayonara."

The monkey and the jellyfish parted on the best of terms. Disappointed the jelly fish returned to the Palace. Meanwhile the Dragon King, the doctor and the chief Steward were all waiting for the Jellyfish to return. When they caught sight of him approaching the Palace they hailed him with delight.

The Jellyfish told all that had to be said. How the monkey had deceived him by saying that it had left the liver behind. To this the Dragon King was furious. He gave orders to punish the Jellyfish. All the bones were drawn out of the body and he was beaten with sticks.

The poor Jellyfish was humiliated and horrified beyond all words as it cried for pardon. After pulling out the bones they beat him to a flat pulp and threw him into the water.

That is why the jellyfish has no bones and has this shape which it has now.

The White Hare and the Crocodiles

Long long ago in the province of Inaba in Japan lived a little White Hare. All the animals could talk in those times. The White Hare lived on the island of Oki just across the mainland of Inaba. The hare wanted to cross over the sea and go to Inaba. Day after day he would look longingly at the water and hoped to find a way to go across.

One day as usual the hare was standing on the beach when he saw a great crocodile swimming near the island.

"Now I shall be able to fulfill my wish," thought the Hare.

"I will ask the crocodile to carry me across the sea." But the hare had its doubts. The crocodile was pleased to see the Hare.

The crocodile persuaded, "You must be lonely Mr. Hare!." Saying this the crocodile came and sat on the shore.

The hare expressed his wish to visit the mainland.

"I know very little about you since I live on the island."

"Do you think the number of your company is greater than mine?" asked the Hare.

The crocodile answered, "There are more crocodiles than hares"

The crocodile was very conceited.

He boasted, "If I call together all the crocodiles who dwell in the sea to the number of hares living on the small island if compared are nothing."

The hare meant to play a trick on the hare.

"Do you think that it is possible to call all the crocodiles to form a line on this island across the sea to Inaba?"

"Then do try," said the artful Hare, "and I will count the number from here!"

The crocodile found it quite easy to carry out the task. The crocodile was very simple and did not see through the trick. It immediately agreed to arrange a line of crocodiles in the water so as to form a bridge between the island of Oki and the mainland of Inaba.

When the hare saw the bridge of crocodiles it stated "Let me count you all and for that I will have to walk over on your backs."

"Please be good as not to move or else I shall drown" suggested the hare.

So, the hare hopped off the island onto the strange bridge of crocodiles counting as it jumped from one crocodile to another. Thus, the cunning hare walked right across to the mainland of Inaba. Not content after getting his wish the hare started to jeer at the crocodiles.

"Oh! you stupid crocodiles, I have done with you." The hare was laughing at them for their stupidity.

And he was just about to run away when the crocodiles understood the trick the hare had played. They became so angry that the crocodiles decided to take revenge. So, some of them ran and caught the hare. Then they surrounded all the hare and pulled out all his fur. The hare cried out loudly and begged the crocodile to spare him but the crocodiles did not feel like giving the hare a pardon.

After pulling out all the hare, they threw the poor hare on the beach and swam away laughing at what they had done.

The hare was now in a pitiful plight and his bad little body was quivering with pain and bleeding all over. The hare could barely move and he could do nothing but helplessly lie on the beach and wept over the misfortune that had befallen him. It was his own fault that had caused him misery for the crocodiles had been very cruel to him.

After some time, the king's men came to the beach and saw the hare and were astonished. They enquired with the hare.

The hare lifted his head and answered," I had a fight with the crocodiles and they pulled out all my fur and left me to suffer."

One of these young men had a bad and spiteful disposition and feigned his kindness.

"I know of a remedy which will cure your sore body. Go and bathe yourself in the sea and then come and sit in the wind. This will make your fur grow again. You will look just as before."

But as the wind blew and dried the fur became hardened and the salt increased the pain so much that the hare rolled on the sand and cried in agony.

Just then another of the king's men passed there and was filled with pity and said," Your hair is pulled out and your skin is bare. Who had treated you like this?"

When the hare heard these words, it was encouraged and told all that had happened. The hare hid nothing from this new friend. The whole story was related and the hare also went on to relate how he had been deceived by a party of men who looked very like this new friend. The hare ended his long tale by begging the man to give the hare some medicine.

The friend replied that the plight of the hare was due to the mistake of the hare himself.

To which the hare said, "I know but I have repented and made up my mind to never use deceit again."

"I beg you to show me how I may cure my sore body and make the fur grow again," said the hare.

The man replied, "Go and bathe in the pond and try to wash all the salt from the body and then pick some of the flowers growing near the edge and and after spreading them on the ground roll yourself on them. If you do this the pollen will help to grow the fur again.

The hare was very glad to be told what to do. He crawled to the pointed pond and bathed well in it and did as it was told. To his amazement even while he was doing this, he saw his nice white fur growing and the pain ceased.

The hare was overjoyed at his quick recovery and went to the young man who had been kind to him and kneeled down on his feet.

"I cannot express enough thanks for all you have done for me! It is my earnest wish to do something for you in return."

"Please tell me who you are?" said the hare.

"I am not anyone from the king but a fairy. Those men who passed here before me are my brothers. They have heard of a beautiful princess called Yakami who lives in this province of Inaba and are on their way to find her and to ask her to marry one of them. I am only an attendant and am walking behind them with this big bag on my back."

The hare was humbled for the fairy many in that part of the land worshiped as a God.

It retorted, "I did not know that you were Okuni-nushi-no-Mikoto. You have been very kind to me. It is impossible to believe that the unkind fellow who told me to bathe in the sea is one of your brothers. I am quite sure that the princess will refuse to marry and be a bride to any of them but will prefer you instead and I am sure that you will easily win her heart with the intention to do so and will ask to be your bride."

Okuni-nushi-no-Mikoto took no notice of what the hare had told and bid the hare a goodbye and went on his way. He quickly overtook his brothers and found them entering a gate.

Just as the hare had declared the princesses could not be persuaded to become the bride of any of the brothers but looked at the kind man who had helped the hare and her heart felt a change.

"To you I give myself" and so they married.

Okuni-nushi-no-Mikoto is worshiped by the people of Japan and the hare is famous as "The White Hare of Inaba." But nobody knows what became of the crocodiles.

The Maiden of Unai

The Maiden of Unai was an earthly and fair deity. She dwelt in a hidden place in her father's house. Nobody knows what cheer she made the whole long day to live. Her father kept watch and her mother kept ward and her ancient nurse tended her.

When the maid was about seven years old with her hair loose and hanging to the shoulders a traveler came with footsore and weary to her father's house. He was made welcome and served rice and tea. The master of the house sat nearby and the mistress did him the honor of serving. Meanwhile the little maid went here and there pattering her bare feet on the mats or bouncing a great green ball in a corner. The stranger marked the child.

After he had eaten, he called for a bowl of clear water and taking from his wallet a handful of silver slipped the money into the bowl. He spoke, "I was hungry and weary and I am a poor man and it is hard to show my gratitude. But I am a soothsayer by profession and famed for my skill of divination. I have looked into the future of your child. Do you want to hear her destiny?"

He continued, "The Maiden of Unai shall grow fairer than any children and her beauty shall shine as the beauty of an earthly deity. Every man who looks upon her will pine with love and when she is fifteen years old there shall die for her sake a hero. And there shall be sorrow and mourning because of her and the sound of it shall reach high heaven and offend the peace of gods."

And with that he bound on his sandals and taking his staff and hat of rice-straw spoke no other word and went his way. Neither was he seen nor heard again.

The father and mother took counsel.

The mother wept, "Who can alter the pattern of doom set upon the women of heaven?"

But the father cried, "I will fight, I will avert the thing for it shall not come to pass of why I am that could give credence to a dog of a soothsayer?"

And though his wife shook her head and moaned, the father gave her no heed for he was a man. So, they hid the child in a secret chamber where an old wise woman tended her, fed her, bathed her, combed her hair and taught her songs and to sing and dance so that her feet moved like butterflies or to do needlework drawing the thread hour after hour.

For eight years the maiden set no eyes on a human being save her father, her mother and her nurse. All day she spent her days lonely and alone far from the sights of the world. But in the night, she came to the garden when the moon shone and the birds slept and the flowers had no Color. And with every season the maid grew more beautiful. Her hair hung to her knees and was black as a thundercloud. Her cheek a wild cherry and her mouth the flower of the pomegranate and thus she was the loveliest thing that one could set eyes upon and therefore the sun was sick with jealousy because only the moonlight could shine upon her.

In spite of all the hiding the fame of her beauty spread far and wide and men desired her more since she was kept hidden and longed to marry her. And all warriors and gallants flocked to the house of Unai and swore that they would not leave the place till they set sight on the maiden which they would get either by favor or by force.

Then the master of the house sent her mother to bring her down. So, the mother went taking with her a robe of silk, a girdle and found her daughter singing thus:

"Nothing has changed since the time of the gods, neither the running of water nor the way of love."

And the astonished mother declared, "What type is the song and where have you come to hear about love?"

And she said, "I have read it in a book."

Then they took her, her mother and the wise woman and tied her hair and pinned it high upon her head with coral pins and declared that it was very heavy. They dressed her in the robe of silk and tied the girdle of brocade to which the maden retorted that she felt cold and it burned.

When they painted her lips with Beni, she murmured that there was blood on her lips. But even then, they led her down to the balcony where the men who assembled might see her. She was very fair and ner beauty shone like that of an earthly deity. And all the warriors fell silent as soon as they saw her. Three or four sought her hand and became distraught but amongst them were two who were nobler than the rest. The first one was the champion of Chinu who came from far and the second was the Champion of Unai who came from near. They were equal in years, strength and valor. Together like twins they stood beneath the balcony and cried aloud with passionate voices telling of their love and persuading the maiden to choose between them. However, the Maiden chose to remain silent.

Her father came to devise a better way to make the right decision. Now part of the house was built on a platform over the river which was swift and deep. While the mother and wise woman hid their faces on their sleeves the maiden stood there itself. Presently a white-water bird dropped from the blue sky and rocked to and fro upon the water.

The father challenged the champions to draw their bows and fly an arrow through the white bird that was floating to and fro on the water. He then declared that the one to strike the bird first would be eligible to wed his daughter.

Then immediately the two warriors let their arrows fly at the bird and each arrow struck true. The champions were angered because the trifle decided that the only way to continue the fight was with their swords. At this the maid was scared and let the flowers of the Wisteria in her hands fall about her.

The maid cried that she loved both of them and swung clear of the balcony and dropped into the deep and swift flowing river and while doing this she wept that no woman dies on that day but it is a child that is lost. And so she sank.

Down sprang the champion of China and down sprang the champion of Unai. But since their arms were heavy with weaponry, they got entangled in the long water weeds and so the three of them drowned.

But as the moon shone there was the glimpse of pale dead rose floating on the water with the champion of Unai holding the Maiden's right hand in his own and the champion of Chinu lay with his head against the Maiden's heart bound close to her with a tress of her long hair and as he lay there he was found smiling.

The three corpses were then lifted from the water and laid on the white wood and over them they strew flowers and herbs and laid a veil over their faces of fine white silk. And they lit fires and burned incense. Warriors who loved the maiden stood by the bier and made a hedge with their swords and mourned and the sound of it offended the gods in heaven.

A grave was dug and three were buried therein with the maid in the middle and the two champions on either side. They brought earth from the native place of the champion of Chinu and covered him with it. And the weapons of artillery were buried with them. The bows of white wood, their armor, their swords and their spears. Nothing was left which was needful for adventure in the land of Yomi.

The Story of the man who did not wish to die

Long long ago there lived a man named Sentaro whose surname meant "millionaire." Although he was not so rich but was far from being poor because he had inherited a small fortune from his father. He lived on the bit of fortune leading his life carelessly without work till he was about thirty-two years of age. One day thoughts of sickness came to him. The idea of falling ill made him wretched. He wanted to live till he was six hundred years old.

"The ordinary span of a man's life is very short." thought the man.

He knew there were many stories in ancient history of emperors who had lived long and there was princess Yamato who was said to have lived till the age of five hundred. Senators had often heard the tale of Shin-no-Shiko who was the most powerful ruler in Chinese history who had built the Great Wall of China. But in spite of all this happiness and splendor of his reign he has the fear of death. It disheartened him from day to night and the thought of death always followed him. He could not get away from it and wanted to find the elixir of life.

The emperor soon called his courtiers and asked them to bring him the elixir of life which he had so often heard about. A courtier by the name Jofuku set out towards the land of Horizon to find the hermits to bring the elixir of water. He was given great quantities of treasures and precious stones to take as presents to the hermits. He sailed away but never returned to the waiting emperor. We must know that Mount Fuji is known to be the land of the hermits and Jofuku is considered ever since as a God.

Sentaro was determined to find the land of the hermits. He remembered that as a child he had been told that these hermits lived on Mount Fuji. So, he left his old home to the care of his relatives, traveled throughout the mountainous regions of the land and climbed the highest peaks but never could find a hermit. But at last after wandering from days he came across a hunter.

"Can you tell me," Asked Sentaro, "where the hermits live who have the elixir of life?"

The hunter denied his request but retorted that he knew of a robber who was the chief of a band of two hundred followers. This answer irritated Sentaro and thought it foolish to continue looking for the hermits. He decided to go at once to the shrine of Jofuku who is worshiped as the patron god of the hermits. Sentaro reached the shrine and prayed for seven days to give him what he wanted. At midnight on the seventh day where Sentaro knelt the door of the shrine flew open and Jofuku appeared in a Cloud and spoke thus:

"Your desire is a selfish one and cannot be easily granted. You think you would like to become a hermit but do you know how hard the life of a hermit is?" enquired Jofuku.

"A hermit is allowed only to eat fruit and berries and his heart must be as pure as gold and free from earthly desire. Thus the hermit ceases to feel hunger or cold and his body becomes so light that he is able to walk on water."

"Moreover you are sensitive to cold and heat and are very lazy" .

"In answer to your prayer however, I will help you in another way. I will send you to the country of life where death never comes and where the people live forever."

Saying this Jofuku gave Sentaro a little bird made of paper which was supposed to carry him there. The bird grew large enough for Sentaro to ride on it and flew away over the mountains and right out to the sea. At first Sentaro was frightened but the bird never stopped and carried Sentaro for thousands of miles.

As the bird was made of paper it didn't require any food and strangely neither Sentaro felt hungry.

After several days they reached an island as the bird landed some distance inland. As soon as Sentaro got down the bird folded itself up and flew into his pocket.

Sentaro was curious to see what the country of Eternal life was like. He walked throughout the town and found everything strange and different from his own land. The people he observed were rich and so he decided to check into one of the hotels.

The hotel owner was a kind man and when Sentaro revealed that he was a stranger the man nodded to arrange all the necessities for his stay by informing the governor of the country. A house was found for Sentaro and he soon became the resident of the country on this land where no man has ever died and sickness was unknown.

Priests who came from China and India told them of a beautiful country called Paradise where happiness filled all the hearts but its gates could only be reached after death. But nobody knew what death was except that it led to paradise.

Quite unlikely the people both rich and poor desired death. They were tired of their long lives and wanted to go to the happy land of contentment about which the priests had told them about a centuries ago.

Sentaro soon found out from talking to the islanders that this town was upside down and the people were topsy and turvy in their beliefs. Sentaro, who had wished to escape death, found that the inhabitants of the island were doomed never to die and considered death as a gift. What food Sentaro considered as poison they ate happily and rejected the food he was used to. Whenever any merchants came by, the rich eagerly bought poisons which they swallowed eagerly hoping for death. But no poison had any effect in this strange land. The people tried to imagine death and felt happy.

There was a drug available which was in constant demand which made the hair go pale and brought disorders of the stomach after constant use. The poisonous fishes were served as dishes in the hotel and sellers sold sauces made of flies in the market. But strangely the people never fell ill.

Sentaro was delighted. He assured himself that he would never grow tired of living such a life of ease and prosperity for such things were like a miracle to him. He thought it crazy to wish for death and became the only happy man on the island.

As years went by, things didn't turn out so smoothly as expected. He recurred heavy losses in business and his neighbors caused him annoyance. Sentaro became busy from morning till night. Soon,

Sentaro longed to see his land and home. He thought it foolish to live here forever?

Sentaro recollected Jofuku who had given him the privilege to live in the land of eternal life. Once again Sentaro prayed to Jofuku to send him back home. No sooner did he start praying the paper bird flew out of his pocket and grew and grew till it was large enough for him to ride on it. The bird flew away with Sentaro carrying him miles across out of the sea to his homeland.

Then a storm occurred and the paper bird was dampened. Sentaro was frightened of being drowned and cried out to Jofuku to save him. There was no ship in sight and Sentaro found himself in a miserable situation. Suddenly he saw a Shark swimming towards him with its huge mouth wide open. Sentaro screamed out so loudly that Jofuku should have heard him.

Sentaro was awakened by his own screams and found that he was alive and had fallen asleep in the shrine while praying. He understood that all his adventures were a dream. He found himself sweating in cold profusion.

Suddenly in front of him stood a messenger with a book in his hand and spoke to Sentaro:

"I am sent to you by Jofuku who has permitted you to see the land of eternal life. But since you wanted to return to your native land Jofuku made you realize the importance of life. He allowed you to drown in your dream even though it was not real so that the true idea of living like a human being would manifest in you. These things like eternal life are not for everyone."

"Never neglect the advice of your ancestors and provide for the future of your children. You must have by now found out that selfish desires such as eternal life are of no use and granted, they don't bring happiness."

A book was handed over to Sentaro which contained some important principles of leading a fruitful life.

Sentaro took the lesson to his heart and with the book returned to his old home giving up all his old desires and tried to live a good life and began to observe the lessons taught to him by the book. Sentaro thus went to lead a meaningful life free of desires of the land of eternal life.

The Happy Hunter and the Skillful Fisher

Long long ago Japan was occupied by Hohodemi, the Augustness in descent from the Amaterasu, the sun goddesses who was not only handsome but beautiful. But he was also strong and known for his bravery and matchless skill as a hunter for he was called Yama-Sachi-hiko or the happy hunter of the mountains. His elder brother who was proficient in fishing was known as Unii-Sachi-Hiko or the skillful fisherman of the sea.

The brothers led a happy life while days passed quickly and pleasantly. One day the hunter brother said to his fisher brother:

I see you go out to the sea with a fishing rod in hand and return with the catch of the day while it is a pleasure for me to take my bow and arrows to hunt wild animals. He proposed that for a long time they had followed their own personal occupations and must be rather tired pursuing it, one of fishing and the other of hunting.

He said, "Would it not be wise for us to make a change?" To which the fisher brother consented. The hunter took his brother's hook and the fisherman took the bow and arrows. It was unwise of them as the hunter knew nothing of fishing and the fisherman was bad tempered and knew nothing of hunting.

The happy hunter went down and sat on the rocks holding the fishing rod and waiting in vain for his luck to turn. At last the evening came but there was not a single fish up to the hook. Drawing up his line for the last time before going home he found that the hook was lost and began to feel anxious. His fisher brother would surely get angry as he values the hook above all other things. The happy hunter set himself the task of finding the hook amongst the rocks. While he was searching for the same the brother arrived on the scene and in a bad temper and when he saw the hunter searching about on the shore, he immediately understood that something was wrong.

"What is happening?" —-what is the matter?

'I have lost the hook," replied the brother.

While he was speaking the fisher brother cried out fiercely that it was just what he had accepted.

He retorted, "As if changing our occupations was not bad enough, you have now lost the hook".

"Who is to be blamed?"

The happy hunter bore this with much humility. He hunted everywhere for the hook which was nowhere to be found.

He then broke his beloved sword into pieces and made five hundred hooks out of it. He took these to his angry brother and asked forgiveness. But it was useless.

"Though you make a million hooks, they are of no use to me." said the fisherman.

Nothing would appease the anger of the fisherman for he hated his brother because of his virtues and with the excuse of the hook planned to kill his brother to usurp his place as the ruler of Japan. The happy hunter knew this well but could do nothing about it. Being the younger he owed his elder brother obedience. So, he returned to the shore and once more began looking for the hook. While he stood on the beach lost in thought on what to do next, an old man suddenly appeared carrying a stick in hand.

"You are what Augustness calls a happy hunter?" enquired the old man.

To this the young man replied with a yes.

'Unfortunately, I lost a hook which was used by my brother. Alas! I cannot find it. I am very disturbed.'

"My name is Shiwozuchino Okina and I live near this shore. I am sorry to hear about the misfortune. You must indeed be anxious. The hook is either at the bottom of the sea or some fish has swallowed it. And for this reason you may never find the hook."

'Thank You,' said the happy hunter.

The old man offered to help the happy hunter. The old man set to work and made a basket and offered it to the hunter which resembled a small boat. The old man pointed out the direction the hunter had to take and taught him the secret of reaching the realm of Ryn Gu.

Riding out on the basket which was given by the old man, the hunter started his journey. The boat was queer and floated on the water of his own accord. The journey was shorter than he had expected and soon reached the Sea king's Palace.

It was a large place with lots of gables and roofs and had huge stonewalls. Leaving his basket on the beach he walked up to a gateway. The gate was very beautiful, made of red coral and was adorned with gems of all kinds.

The hunter hero who held the knowledge about the palace fell short of praise to the reality he now faced.

As he came near the hunter noticed that the gate was closed. In the shade of the trees before the gate he caught sight of a well full of fresh water. Then he climbed into the tree overhanging the well and seated himself on one of the branches and waited for something to happen.

He didn't have to wait for long as the gate opened soon and two beautiful women came out. The happy hunter had heard that Ryn Gu was the realm of the Dragon King and the place was inhabited by several such monsters.

He didn't speak a word but silently watched on through the foliage. He saw that the women carried golden buckets in their hands. As the two ladies leaned over to the side they saw reflected in the deep water the face of a handsome youth gazing at them. As they had not seen the face of a mortal man they were frightened. However their curiosity aroused them to go near the hunter.

When the happy hunter saw that he was discovered he lied, "I am a traveler who is very thirsty. Therefore, I pray for you to quench my thirst."

The woman overruled their fears because of the dignity of the hunter and letting down their buckets drew water from the well, pouring the water into a cup and offering it to the hunter.

The happy hunter received the water and raised it high above his head as a token of respect and drank the water for his thirst was great. After that, drawing his sword, cut off one of the jewels hanging from his necklace, placed it in the cup and returned it to them falling abreast.

The two ladies finding the gem stone gave a start of surprise for they had failed to realize the capacity of the hunter.

They introduced themselves to be the daughters of Ryn Jin, the king of the Sea.

The hunter went on, "The other day I had lost a hook which I had taken from my brother. Unless I find it again, I can never hope to win my brother's forgiveness. I met an old man who told me to find Ryn Gu and go to Ryn Jin, the Dragon king of the sea."

"Will you be kind enough to take me to your father?"

Princess Tayotama listened to this long story and said:

"Not only is it easy for you to see my father but it is also easy for you to find your fortune. A great and noble man as you, the grandson of Amaterasu, should come to the bottom of the sea."

"Condescend to enter Mikoto, the happy hunter."

The younger sister reached the palace first and quickly ran to her father to tell him if the guest. The Dragon King of the sea was surprised at the news for it was seldom perhaps in a hundred years that the Sea king's palace was visited by mortals.

Ryn Jin dressed himself in ceremonious robes and went to welcome the hunter. The Sea King then led the happy hunter to the guest room.

The hunter bowed respectfully, "Are you indeed the king of sea? I must apologize for the trouble I have given you."

Ryn Jin then went on "It is I who must thank you for coming."

There was much gladness between the Sea King and the Happy hunter. The Sea King served the hunter with a lot of delicious fish delights. A great feast was spread before the king and his royal guest. All in the palace did their best to please him and to show him that they were honored. The two princesses came in and performed on the KOTO, a Japanese harp and danced to its tunes. The time passed so pleasantly that the happy hunter seemed to forget his trouble and gave himself up to the enjoyment of the palace.

But the hunter soon returned to his query, "May I ask you to be so kind as to inquire on all subjects if any of them have seen a fishing hook lost in the sea?"

"I will immediately summon all of them and ask them," retorted the king.

On his command the Octopus, the Cuttlefish, the Bonito, the Oxtail Fish, the Eel, the JellyFish, the Shrimp, and many other fishes of all kinds came in and sat down before Ryn Jin.

The Sea King said solemnly, "Our visitor sitting before you is the grandson of Amaterasu. His name is Hohodemi the fourth Augustness and he is also called the happy hunter of the mountains. He has lost his brother's fishing hook. He has come all the way to the bottom of the sea looking for the hook which one of your fishes have stolen in mischief. If any of you have borrowed the hook, please return it immediately."

All the fishes were taken by surprise but the cuttlefish came forward and disclosed that, "I think the TAI must be the one who has stolen it."

"Since yesterday evening the TAI has not been able to eat anything and seems to be suffering from a bad throat. The hook must be inside the throat. And it is strange that the TAI has not obeyed your summons."

The King wanted the TAI to be presented to the court at once. And the TAI sat there looking frightened.

They responded, "I have been ill since yesterday."

"The hook is still in my throat. I cannot eat and can scarcely breathe. I snapped at the bait which I saw in the water and the hook came off and stuck in my throat."

"Please hurry and pull it out," cried the TAI.

Then after opening the mouth of the TAI, the cuttlefish with their feelers easily drew the hook out and brought it to the king.

Ryn Jin took the hook from the subject and then respectfully returned it to the king. The hunter was overjoyed with gratitude to get his hook back. Ryn Jin wanted to punish the TAI who had taken the hook but what had been done was in heedlessness and not by intention.

The Happy Hunter but blamed himself. If he had only understood how to fish properly, he would not have suffered. So, the TAI was forgiven.

Now that the hook was found the happy hunter was anxious to get back to his kingdom and to make peace with his brother. The two lovely princesses however pressed him to stay and make the palace his home.

Three years went fleeting quickly and the Happy Hunter failed to realize the advent of time. The kindness of the Sea King however seemed to grow. But the Happy Hunter soon got homesick.

He explained to the King thus, "I am very grateful for your kindness. But I must return the hook to my brother.I now must take your leave."

King Ryn Jin was overcome with sorrow.

He replied, "You have been a noble guest. We would like you to stay. I Hope you will remember us. Let the friendship that has begun between the land and Sea grow stronger."

However, the Sea King ordered his daughters to present the Happy Hunter with a gift. Each one returned carrying a flashing gem that filled the room with light.

He further conceded, "I am gifting you these two Talismans which have been inherited by us from our ancestors."

'I can never thank you enough,' replied the Happy Hunter.

'Tell me what these jewels are and what I am to do with them?' the Hunter bowed.

"These two gems are called the Nanjiu and the Kanjiu. The Nanjiu or the jewel of the Flood tide has the power to roll the Sea and to flood the land at any time. The Kanjiu or the jewel of the Ebbing tide controls the waves and also causes them to recede.

The Happy Hunter was very glad to receive these gifts as he felt that they would save him from danger. And after a Goodbye the Happy Hunter passed out from under the gateway and went past the well of Happy memory standing in the shade of the great KATSURA and went back to the beach.

Here instead of the queer basket on which he had come he found a Crocodile waiting. And he had never seen such a large crocodile in his life. The Sea King ordered the creature to carry the Hunter back to his land.

The Skillful Fisher who had not heard the news of his brother being alive had usurped his brothers place as a ruler and had become powerful and rich. However, he feigned forgiveness and day after day planned and watched for an opportunity to kill him.

One day when the Hunter was walking through the fields his brother followed him with a dagger. But the Hunter was well aware of the plan. It was time to use the Jewels. He took the Jewel of the Flood Tide and raised it to his head and instantly the Sea came rolling in and reached the spot where his brother was standing to which the Fisher was terrified and soon was struggling in the water to save his life.

The Happy Hunter had a kind heart and could not bear the distress. The Hunter therefore raised the Jewel of the ebbing tide to his forehead and the Sea ran back. The tossing waves vanished and the dry fields soon appeared.

The Skillful Fisher was greatly impressed by these wonderful things of magic. He Humbled himself before the hunter and asked him to forgive for the wrong he had done. The Fisher promised to restore the rights of the Hunter.

The Skillful Fisher exalted him as superior and swore allegiance to him. The Happy Hunter put down the condition that the Fisher would only be forgiven if he would throw into the receding tide all his evil ways. The Skillful Fisher kept his promise and became a good man.

The Happy Hunter ruled the land of Japan happily for a long long time to come with prosperity and glory.

The Tale of the Bamboo Cutter

Long long ago there lived a bamboo wood cutter who was poor and childless due to which he always remained sad. He had no rest from his work. Every morning, he went into the woods where bamboo grew and made his choice to cut down these rewards of the forest. Then he split them lengthwise and carried the bamboo home out of which he made articles fit for the household and sold them for his livelihood.

One morning as usual he went to work and found a nice clump of Bamboos. The groove was suddenly flooded with light. He looked around and found that the light was coming from one of the bamboo. On going nearer, he understood that the soft splendor came from a hollow in the stem. In the midst of this bamboo was a tiny human being who was very beautiful in appearance.

The bamboo cutter thought, "You must be a gift for me directly from the heavens".

Collecting the little creature in his hands he took it home to his wife. The tiny girl was unexpectedly beautiful and small. The woman put her into a basket to safeguard her.

The old couple were now very happy since they had no children of their own and were filled with joy because of this treasure which had arrived at their home.

From that day fortune smiled upon the bamboo cutter. He found precious stones and gold hidden in the notches of the Bamboos. Due to this he soon became rich and built himself a fine house.

Three months passed and the Little girl became a beautiful grown-up girl. Her parents dressed her in a lovely Kimono and did her hair. She was so lovely that they placed her behind a screen and did not allow anyone to see her. She was made of light and the whole house was filled with her shine. The dark of the night seemed like sunshine. Her presence had a benign influence on those around her. The old man was happy with this and felt rejuvenated.

At last a day came when they had to give a name to the child. So, the couple called in a celebrated name giver who gave her the name of Princess Moonlight because of the bright light she illuminated and had a hunch that she was the daughter of the Moon God.

All the friends and relations of the couple were called for the naming ceremony and for three days the festival was kept up with music and dance. Everyone was impressed by the tiny human as they had never seen such beauty throughout the length and breadth of the land. The fame of the beauty of the princesses spread far and wide.

Suitors from far and near asked for her hand. They stood outside the house hoping to catch a glimpse of Princess moonlight. They stayed there day and night even sacrificing their sleep but in vain. So, at last they approached the old man and his wife but could do nothing.

So great was their desire to see the princesses that they stayed there day after day and night after night.

But at last some men felt hopeless and went back to their home. All except five knights who were so determined that they went without their meals and took whatever was brought to them so that they may catch a glimpse of the Princess. They stood there itself in the sun and in the rain.

They also wrote letters to the princesses but they went unanswered. And when these letters failed to get attention, they began writing poems giving the princesses proof about their hopeless love. This kept them from falling asleep, lack of food and from rest. But Princesses Moonlight didn't seem to register their verses.

In this hopelessness winter came upon them. The snow gave way to cold winds and that gave gradually a way to the gentle warmth of the spring. Then the summer came, which was scorching and bright. But the faithful knights kept on with their watch. At the end of these long months, they called out to the old bamboo cutter and told him to show some consideration to which the old man gave the excuse that he was not her real father.

The five knights therefore returned to their homes to ponder over a solution. They knelt before the shrines, burning incense praying to Buddha to grant them their desire.

After this they again set out to the Bamboo cutter's house. But this time the old man came outside to see them. They implore him to speak and tell the princesses the greatness of their love towards her. The time they had spent standing outside the house in the cold winter and scorching summer in the hope of winning her hand. And they were willing to rule these out if she could give them one chance of seeing her face.

The old man was now willing for he felt sorry for them and their love and their faithfulness.

So, he went to Princess Moonlight and pleaded, "You seem to me to have come directly from the heavens and I have looked after you like my own child. I also had to bear the trouble of attending to you."

Princess Moonlight replied that he was like her real father and that she loved him even more to which the old man listened with great joy.

He proposed further, "Would you see the five knights and decide upon a suitor?"

The princess however replied that she had no wish to marry.

"I found you many years ago in the midst of divine light till you became a woman. You can remain as you are but one day I shall cease to be and I am afraid that you shall lose yourself in the being. Therefore, it is my plea that you meet these five brave men and make up your mind to marry one of them."

To this the princesses retorted that she was not beautiful as the old man thought and even if she consented to marry one of them their heart might change afterwards.

At this the old man consented, "You are being reasonable but who these knights have waited upon you for months just to get a glimpse of you. What more can you demand?"

The princesses moonlight told that she wanted to make further trial of their love and requested to interview the knights

They had to travel around the world and bring her something interesting. The bamboo cutter gave them this message with great sympathy in his heart. This was to test them.

The five knights thought of it as an excellent plan because it would prevent jealousy from emerging between them.

She requested the first Knight to bring the stone-bowl which had belonged to Buddha in India. The second Knight was asked to go to the mountain of Horai and bring a branch of the wonderful tree that grew in the summit. The roots of this tree were silver, the trunk gold and branches bore jewels. The third knight was told to go to China and search for the fire rat and bring the skin. The fourth Knight was said to search for the Dragon and to bring the stone on its head which radiated five colors. The fifth Knight was asked to bring the swallow which carried a shell in its stomach.

The Knights felt disgusted after hearing the words of the old man and were disheartened about the tasks they had to carry out. But the love they held in their hearts for her was greater. And so, the first Knight sent his word that he was going to carry out the task set on him.

In those days traveling was considered to be dangerous. He went to one of the temples in Kyoto and took a stone bowl from the altar there after paying the priest heavily for the same. He then wrapped it in a cloth of gold and after waiting for a period of further three years carried it to the old man.

The princesses took the bowl in her hand but it failed to light the house and didn't shine. She therefore understood that the gift was not real. She returned the bowl and refused the First Knight who returned to his home in despair and gave up all hopes of winning the hand of the Princesses.

The Second Knight told his parents that he needed a change of air for his health because he was totally engrossed in his love for the princess and was ashamed to tell them that his love for the princesses was the real cause of his leaving. He also sent word to the princesses that he was set for the task assigned to him. He allowed his servants to accompany him half way and sent them back. After sailing away for three days he landed and employed some carpenters to build him a house. He then shut himself in the house with six skilled jewelers and told them to make such a branch of gold and silver which he thought could satisfy the Princesses. Then he went home making himself look weary and worn out presenting the branch in a lacquer box begging the old man to present it to the princesses.

The Old man persuaded the princesses to see the Knight for he was deceived by the appearance of the Knight. The old man praised it as a wonderful treasure to be found nowhere else in the world. But the Princess understood that the branch was artificial. It was impossible that the branch was from the mountain of Horai.

The Knight being questioned made up a story.

"Two years ago, I started on the trip and after facing the wind reached the far eastern sea and then a great storm arose and I was tossed for many days but was finally blown ashore on an unknown island. It was inhabited by demons who threatened to eat me. However, I made friends with them and they helped me repair my boat. But our food gave out and me and my sailors suffered from sickness. On the five hundredth day from the day of starting we came upon the mountain. I saw a shining being coming towards me holding a golden bowl in my hand who confirmed that it was Mount Horai. With much difficulty I climbed to the summit and there I found the golden tree with silver roots and after breaking a branch I hurried back. It took me four hundred days to get back and my clothes are still damp from exposure."

But just at this moment, those who had been employed on making the branch arrived at the house and sent in a petition to be paid for their labor. They said that they had worked a thousand days in making the branch and had yet to receive payment.

The Princess was only pleased to send the branch back. She called in the workmen who were paid liberally and went home. But on the way the depressed Knight overtook them and beat them up heavily. The Knight thus retired to a solitary life among the mountains in despair of ever winning the hand of the princesses.

Now, the third Knight had a friend in China. He wrote to him to get the skin of a fire-rat. The virtue of this animal was that no fire could harm it. The friend was promised a handsome amount of money. The friend came home to the port and when he did, the Knight rode seven days on horseback to reach him to receive the fire-rats skin and paid him heavily.

The bamboo cutter on receiving the box containing the skin tried to coax the princesses to see the Knight. Princess Moonlight wanted to check the authenticity of the product. She took off the wrapper and opened the box. She then proceeded to throw it into the fire. The skin burnt up at once and the princess understood that this man also was not telling the truth. The third Knight had failed.

The number of the fourth Knight came up and instead of starting out on the quest he called all his servants together and gave them the order to seek far and wide for it in Japan and China. His servants started out in different directions however without the intention of carrying out the order. They took a holiday grumbling at their master's unreasonableness.

The Knight meanwhile had started preparations for his reception with the princess. However, after a year of waiting the Knight became desperate. Taking only two men with him he hired a ship and commanded the captain to go in search of the Dragon. But the men refused and the Knight was determined to give up the hunt for the Dragon. They were blown on shore and worn out with his travels and anxiety; the fourth suitor gave up like the rest because he had caught a cold.

The governor of the place after hearing this story sent messengers with a letter inviting him to his house. The Knight after thinking over everything became angry with the princess. He blamed her for all the hardships he had encountered. At this point all the servants who had gone on a holiday came to him and were surprised to find praise and not displeasure awaiting them for the Knight told them that he never wanted to even hear of the Princess again.

But this time the fame of the beauty of princesses moonlight had reached the emperor. He sent one of the court ladies to see if she was really lovely as it was told. He wanted to take her as a lady in waiting. But Princesses Moonlight refused to see her and threatened to vanish from the earth.

When the emperor came to hear of this he was determined to go and see her for himself. So, he planned to go on a hunting excursion in the neighborhood of the Bamboo cutter's house and sent a note to the old man of his intention. The next day the emperor set out and found the house of the old man and dismounted there.

Never had he seen someone so beautiful. When Princess Moonlight became aware of his presence she tried to escape from the room. By now the emperor had fallen for her and begged her to come to the court. He wanted to take the princesses back in an Imperial palanquin for he believed that her grace and beauty should adorn a court.

The princess was angry and told the emperor that she would turn into a shadow. Even as she spoke the figure of the princess began to fade because of which the emperor was forced to retrace his steps. He bade her a goodbye and left with a sad heart. Princess Moonlight had become the most beautiful woman in the world for him. He spent much of his time writing poems which gave him a distant pleasure. But the Princess still refused to see him.

As days passed, her foster parents noticed that night after night the princesses felt dejected and the old man one day caught her weeping in which the princess disclosed the truth that she had come from the moon and her time on earth would soon be over. On the fifteenth day of that August her friends would come to fetch her. She had forgotten her parents and the moon world to which she belonged. It made her weep to leave her kind foster-parents behind. Her attendants after hearing the news left eating. The news also was carried to the emperor who in turn sent his messengers to enquire. The old man weeping bitterly told them that the news was true. He intended to make the envoys from the moon his prisoners and would do all that could prevent the princesses from being carried back.

The emperor then sent a guard of two thousand warriors to watch the house. A thousand stationed themselves on the roof and another thousand kept watch on the entrance. All of them were trainee archers. Meanwhile the bamboo cutter and his wife had hidden the Princess in an inner room. Nobody was to sleep that night even as the princesses told them that all the measures, they had taken would be useless.

The princesses had learnt to love her foster-parents and would live with them if she was allowed to do anything that she pleased and would not be deterred from showering love upon them during all her earthly life.

Silence reigned over the pine and the bamboo forests as the thousand men on the roof awaited arms at hand. Then the night grew gray and all hoped that the danger was over.

Then suddenly the watchers saw a cloud form around the moon which was coming hurtling towards the earth. To the dismay of the people gathered there understood that the target of the cloud was the house.

As the cloud came nearer the sky was obscured and the cloud lay only ten feet over the ground where the house stood. A flying chariot with a band of luminous beings stepped out of the chariot and one amongst them who appeared to be the king called out to the old man to come out.

He called out, "The time has come for the princesses to return to the moon from where she has come and belongs."

"She was sent down to the earth as a sort of punishment for committing a crime."

"We have aptly rewarded you for the same purpose with wealth and prosperity. The gold in the Bamboo was placed as a reward for taking care of the Princesses."

To this the old man replied, 'The lady you are seeking may not be this one for I have brought up the princesses and see no fault in her.'

But the princess was led by the messenger and placed on the chariot to be taken away.

She looked at the old man and spoke a few comforting words and told him that it was not her will to leave him.

The bamboo cutter implored to the heavens to allow him to accompany his daughter to which the princess gifted a piece of cloth that she was wearing to the old man as a keepsake.

The princess was given a wonderful coat to wear which was made of wings and a phial containing the elixir of life.

The princess expressed her desire to say goodbye to her old friend the emperor before she drank the elixir and was still in human form. She wrote a letter to the emperor and as a gift handed over the pot containing the elixir of life to the old man and asked him to deliver it to the emperor.

Slowly the chariot began rolling heaven wards to the moon and as the people gazed dawn broke and in the hazy light, they could make out the teary eyes of the princess. And after that the chariot was lost amongst the clouds that wafted across the sky by the morning wind.

Princess Moonlight's letter was carried to the emperor who was afraid to drink the elixir of life and sent it with the letter to the sacred Mount Fuji where the royal emissaries burnt it at sunrise. To this day people see smoke rising from the top of Mount Fuji to the clouds.

The Crab and the Monkey

Once upon a time in the lush green forest by the river there lived a very clever monkey who was also very naughty. The monkey spent his days swinging from tree to tree and by playing tricks on the animals of the forest thus also enjoying the bountiful fruits of the forest.

One day as the monkey was exploring the river bank he came across a crab scuttling along the shore. The curiosity of the monkey sparked a trigger.

The monkey greeted, "Mr. Crab would you like to be my friend?"

"We can have fun and share the delicious fruits of the forest together."

The Crab was a very wise and careful animal.

'I would be honored to be your friend.'

But since you live on the land and I live on the water, it is highly impossible for us to share fruits from the trees together.

To this the monkey was confused. It scratched his head and suddenly an idea struck the monkey.

The monkey retorted that it would carry the crab on his back so that they could pluck the fruits from the trees together.

It also hinted that they could divide the fruits equally between them.

However, as time passed the nature of the monkey soon began to take hold. One day as they were dividing the fruits between themselves the monkey secretly decided to deceive the Crab.

But the Crab understood the trickery as it had keen eyes and senses. Soon, a feeling of betrayal got hold of the crab.

"My dear friend, it seems that today you have not divided the fruits equally as agreed."

"This is not fair and goes against the spirit of our friendship," the crab disclosed.

"Let us return to the forest and gather more fruits," the monkey replied determinedly.

The Crab displaying forgiveness and wisdom agreed to give their friendship another chance.

Together they ventured back into the forest and this time managed to gather a large amount of fruit. The monkey sincerely swore to divide the fruits equally and handed them over to the crab thus ensuring fairness and harmony between them.

From that day the Monkey and the Crab are steadfast friends. They had learned the importance of honesty, trust and the consequence of greed.

They shared their harvests together and enjoyed the fruits of the forest thus embodying the true spirit of friendship.

The Crab and the Monkey is a timeless tale teaching the valuable lessons of trust and faith instilled in the spirit of friendship and with that the consequences of betrayal.

It serves as a reminder to the children to treat others with kindness and integrity for true friendship is always built on trust, honesty and mutual respect.

Mandarin Ducks

In ancient Japan in a lagoon near what is now Maizuru, north of Kyoto lived a pair of Mandarin ducks. It was spring and they had recently hatched their eggs and the male still held its spectacle with his dark orange beard, his green, blue and red plume and his bill the color of coral which it exhibited before his mate and offspring as well as mandarin ducks would do.

At the same time a young samurai and his wife built their house on the banks of the lagoon. The samurai had not yet entered into the service of the feudal lord. He had not made enough money to buy the traditional attire of a samurai even though it was his profession. The attire could not also be bought as his wife was pregnant. It would have to wait. But the samurai still kept happy and cheerful knowing that he was going to be a father.

One evening his wife told him that she felt an irresistible need to eat meat.

"I know that we don't have enough money to buy meat," retorted the samurai.

"I don't want to disappoint you," he gathered to say.

Later that night when the wife had fallen asleep, he got out of his bed and went hunting. He went to the nearby forest and finding no prey chose to hide in the cane field on the shore of the lagoon hoping to catch a bird.

And sure, enough he caught sight of a male mandarin drake emerging from the hollow of a tree. It made a perfect target. The Samurai shot his arrow and then felled the drake, put it in his sack and returned home, hung the sack on his tree and went back to bed.

Just as he was about to fall asleep a strange sound woke him up. It sounded like the beatings of wings.

The samurai thought that the duck was still alive, got up again and with a knife left the cabin.

To his surprise he discovered that the sound was not from the duck he had hunted but from a female duck who was perched on a branch above the sack where its mate hung. She was fluttering her wings in an useless attempt to bring her mate back to life.

Now, what came to the mind of the samurai was to kill the female duck too in order to gather more meat. But, when he approached the duck the female showed no fear and kept fluttering her wings over the body of the male as if in a strange ritual of mourning.

At this moment, a very deep feeling seized the young samurai, an overwhelming compassion that would never go away and a feeling that could not be easily dismissed. With tears in his eyes he returned to the cabin, woke up his wife and told her all that had happened. The moving display of love the female duck held for her husband.

The wife replied, "I am sorry about the meat."

"I simply cannot eat the Duck now for anything in the world."

And in the Zen Buddhist sanghas it is said that the young man did not complete his process to become a samurai. They said the compassion the young man felt for the mandarin duck transformed his view of reality and after that event he dedicated his life to protect all animals. After his death the man was given the distinguished position of a sage.

The Old Woman who lost her Dumpling.

Long ago there lived a funny old woman who liked to laugh a lot and to make dumplings of rice flour

One day when she was preparing some dumplings for dinner, one of them rolled into a hole in the earthen floor of her little kitchen. The old woman tried to gather the dumpling by putting her hand down the hole but the earth there gave way and the woman fell right inside the hole for quite a distance. She was not hurt even though she did a survey of her surroundings.

She saw that she was standing on a road which was just like the road before her house. She could see plenty of rice fields but there was nobody visible to the eyes.

It seemed that the old woman had fallen into another country.

The road she was on was highly sloped. After having looked for her dumpling in vain, she thought that it had further rolled down the slope.

She ran down the road crying for her dumpling. After a little while she saw a stone standing by the roadside and asked

—- "O' Lord, have you seen my dumpling?"

It answered that a dumpling was rolling down the road and also told her about a wicked Oni living down the road who ate people.

To this the old woman gave a laugh and ran further down the road crying, "My dumpling, my dumpling!"

And then she came to another statue of the stone Lord and asked– "O'kind Lord, did you see my dumpling?"

And it answered—

"Yes, I saw your dumpling go a little while ago. But you must not run further because there is a wicked Oni down there who eats people."

But to that she only laughed now crying out even more urgently, "Where is the dumpling of mine?"

And meanwhile she came upon the third statue of the stone Lord and asked it—

"O'dear Lord, did you see my dumpling?"

But the statue of the lord replied—

"Don't talk about your dumpling because an Oni is on its way now. Please squat behind my sleeve and don't make any noise."

Presently the Oni came very close and stopped and bowed to the lord and uttered—

"Good day"

The Stone Lord also gave the same greeting very politely

But the Oni snuffed the air two or three times in a suspicious way and cried out—

"I smell of mankind somewhere."

To this the statue replied–

"You are mistaken."

— "No. No!" said the Oni after sniffing the air again," I smell the smell of mankind."

Then suddenly the old woman could not help laughing and the Oni immediately reached down his big hairy hand behind the stone Lord's sleeve and pulled out the old woman who was still laughing.

"What are you going to do to the Woman?"

"Please don't hurt the woman" requested the stone Lord.

The Oni replied that he was not going to hurt the old woman but was going to make her cook for him.

The stone Lord retorted, "Be kind to the old woman for I will be angry with you if you hurt her."

The Oni promised— "I won't hurt her but she has to cook for me everyday."

Then the Oni took the old woman far down the road, till they came to a wide deep river, where there was a boat. He put her into the boat and took her across the river to his house.

It was a very large house. He led her to the kitchen and told her to cook dinner for himself and the other Oni who lived with him.

"You must always put one grain of rice into the pot and when you stir that one grain of rice into the water with a paddle the grain will multiply until the pot is full."

So, the old woman just put one grain of rice into the pot and began to stir it with a paddle. One grain became two, then four and then eight—sixteen, thirty two, sixty four and so on.

Every time she moved the paddle the rice increased in quantity and in a few minutes the pot was full.

After that the funny old woman stayed a long time in the house and cooked for the Oni everyday. In return the Oni never hurt or frightened her. Although she had to cook a great quantity of rice because Oni's eat more than what a human being eats.

But she was lonely and always wished to go back to her own house and make dumplings. And one day when the Oni went out she tried to run away.

She first took the magic paddle and slipped it under her girdle. And then she went down the river. She got into the boat and pushed off with the paddle as she could row very well and was soon far away from the shore.

But the river was very wide and she had not rowed more than one-fourth of the way across when the Oni was back to his house.

They found the old woman missing with the Magic paddle. They ran down to the river at once and saw the old woman rowing away very fast.

They could not swim and had no boat, so the only way to catch the funny old woman was to drink up all the water of the river before she got to the other bank. The old woman had gone only half a way when the water level became quite low. But the old woman kept rowing until the Oni had stopped drinking and began to wade across. She dropped her oar and took the magic paddle from her girdle and shook it at the Oni making funny faces till they burst out laughing.

The moment the Oni laughed, the water was thrown up till the river filled itself and had become full again. The funny old woman got safely to the other side and ran away up the road as fast as she could and didn't stop running until she found herself at home again.

After that she was very happy as she could make dumplings whenever she pleased. Besides, she had the magic paddle to make rice for her. She sold her dumplings to her neighbors and passengers and in quite a short time became rich.

The Spring Lover and the Autumn Lover

This is a story of the youth of Yamato when the gods still walked upon the land of the Reed Plains and took pleasure in the countryside.

There was a lady who was made something of earth and something of heaven for she was a king's daughter. She was so majestically beautiful and radiant that she acquired the tiles like the Dear Delight of the world, Greatly Desired or the Fairest of the Fair.

She was both slender and strong and at once mysterious and gay but gentle and hard to please. The gods loved her and other men worshiped her.

Prince Ama Boko had an exquisite red jewel acquired from one of his enemies which was actually a peace offering. He set it in a casket upon a stand and the jewel was transformed into a fair lady, the Lady of the Red Jewel whom he took to be his wife. And born to them was a daughter who was the Greatly Desired and the Fairest of the Fair. Many came to seek her hand and amongst the eighty men some were warriors and some were deities. They came from near and far, across the sea in great ships with white sails or creaking oars with other sailors who were brave. And thus, they crossed dangerous forests making their way to the princess. They descended the Floating Bridge in garments of glamor and silver shod and brought with them gifts of gold and fair jewels upon a string. Also, they brought with them light garments of feathers, singing birds, sweets, silk cocoons and oranges in a basket. Also, they came with minstrels, dancers and story tellers to entertain the princess Greatly Desired.

The Princess sat still in her white bower with maidens wearing a rich robe which spread all over the mats setting out her deep sleeves and combed her long hair with a golden comb. About the bower was a gallery of white wood and the suitors gathered there to catch a glimpse of the lady. As many a time the carp leapt up in the Fish pond and many a times a pomegranate flower fluttered and dropped from a tree which despised the lady for shaking her head and being rejected as a suitor.

It happened that the God of Autumn wanted to try his luck and marry the princess. He was a brave young man with ardent eyes, flamed dark cheeks and carried a sword that ten men could not lift. The chrysanthemums of Autumn burned upon his coat with a good display of embroidery. He came and bent his head down on the ground before the princess, then raised it and looked her full in the eyes to which she said nothing but shook her head.

The God of Autumn blinded wrought bittersweet tears and came upon his younger brother the God of Spring who enquired on how the former one was faring.

"I'll for she has rejected me," replied the God of Autumn.

"She is proud and I have begot a broken heart."

"Come home with me for everything is over."

The God even though decided to stay and related that he would like to visit the princess at least once.

The God of Autumn cried out–

"If you win her i will pay for the wedding feast but if you lose her take no grief but pass her on to me."

The God of Spring thought for a little while and remarked that he would accept the wager.

He turned his head to his mother and asked, "Do you love me, my mother?"

She answered, "More than a hundred exist."

He ventured," Get me for my wife the princess the Fairest of the Fair for she is greatly Desired and I desire her greatly."

So, she spread a couch for him and asked him to sleep and said, "I will work for you because your face is the sweetest thing in the world."

She went to a place where the Wistaria drooped over a still pool and plucked the tendrils and brought it home as much as she could for the Wistaria was white and purple yet hidden the likes of an unopened bud.

From it she wove a robe, fashioned sandals also making some Bow and arrows and in the morning after waking up a spring put the robe on him.

The God of spring accepted the robe and did as his mother bade him, bound the sandals on his feet, slung the bow and the arrows in a quiver and set sail.

So, the God of spring after receiving the blessings of his mother came before the Fairest of the Fair.

One of her maidens laughed, "Here comes another little Plain boy in gray."

But the Fairest of the Fair lifted her eyes and looked upon the God of Spring. At the same moment the Wistaria with which he was clothed burst into a flower and he was garnered with flowers white and purple from head to heel.

To this the princess rose from the mats.

"I am yours if you will have me," she said.

Hand in hand they went to the mother of the God of the spring.

The mother implored, "Be still and fear not."

She took a cane of bamboo which was hollow and put salt and stones in it, wrapped the cane with leaves and hung it in the smoke of the fire.

She said: "The green leaves fade and die. So, my eldest born the God of Autumn you must sink and you must fail like the Ebb tide."

The tale ends here and the readers must have understood that the Spring is fresh and young but Autumn is sad.

The Flute

Long ago there lived in Yedo, a gentleman of high lineage. She was a gentle and loving lady but bore him no sins. But at last a daughter was born to them who was interpreted as "Rice in the ear." They loved her and she was the apple of their eye. The child grew up red and white, straight and slender like the bamboo.

When O'Yone was twelve years old her mother became sick and soon died. The husband was grief stricken. He cried out loud, beat his breast and lay near her on the ground where she was buried. He refused comfort and neither broke his fast nor slept. The child fell silent.

Time passed and the snow of winter covered her grave. The pathway from the grave to the dwelling of his house also was covered with snow save for the imprints of a child's sandalled feet. During the spring the father gathered his robe in order to see the cherry blossom after writing a poem on paper which he hung on the tree to a branch which fluttered in the wind. The poem described the spring in full praise. Later, there itself he planted the Lily of Forgiveness on the ground where his wife lay buried and no longer wished to think of her. But the child remembered.

Before the year ended, he brought a new wife home. But she was a woman with a fair face and a black heart. The man was fooled by his wife and began to care less about the child.

The stepmother hated O'Yone but her father still loved her very much.

One day he called her and said," What gift shall I bring you from Kyoto?"

But she hung her head and did not answer.

Thinking that the child was rude he asked–

"Answer little one whether it will be a red brocade, a roll of silk or a golden fan or a great battledore with images?"

The child started weeping and hid her face on the sleeves and with a broken heart cried, "Father don't go away and take me with you."

The father was surprised and retorted whether she would ride on a horse or walk on foot and how she would fare in the inns of Kyoto being a pilgrim.

"For a little time stay with your kind mother."

The little child thought about this and shuddered.

"Father, if you go, you will never see me anymore."

The father felt a sudden chill about his heart but dismissed it. He was not going to be fooled by the fancies of a child to which O'Yone slipped away as silently as a shadow.

But in the morning, she came to him with a little foot in her hand fashioned of bamboo and smoothly polished.

"I made it from the bamboo growing in the garden."

"As you cannot take me, take this flute with you."

Then she wrapped it in a kerchief lined with Scarlet and wound a Scarlet cord around it and gave it to her father who put it in his sleeve.

After this he departed and went on his way to Kyoto. As he went, he looked back thrice and beheld his child standing near the gate. The road turned after that and she saw him no more.

The city of Kyoto was beautiful as the father of O'Yone found it and what with his business during the day which sped well and his pleasure in the evening and his sound sleep at night the time passed merrily and he gave no thought to Yedo, his child and his home. Two moons passed and three and he made no plans for his return.

One day he wanted to go to a supper of his friends and as he searched in his chest for a silk hakama which he intended to wear as an honor, he came upon the flute which lay hidden all this time on the sleeve of his dress. He drew it from its red and white handkerchief and as he did so felt a strange chill creep across his heart. He put the flute to his lips when he drew from it a long wail.

He dropped it hastily and clapped for his servant and told him that he would not go out for the night as he was not well. He once again heard the wail as he reached out to touch the flute and blew into the flute.

"Come back to Yedo...father! Father!"

The quavering childish voice rose to a shriek and then broke. A horrible foreboding now took hold of the man. He journeyed day and night denying himself sleep and food. So pale was he that the people deemed him as a madman and fled from him and pitied him as afflicted by the gods. At last traveled stained from head to heel with bleeding feet came to Yedo.

His wife met him near the gate.

He asked, "Where is the child?"

"The child...?" she answered.

"Where is She?" he cried in agony.

The Woman only laughed. She is in the garden or maybe she is asleep there or is playing with her playmates.

He said: "Enough;no more of this. Come, where is my child?"

Then she was afraid and replied, "In the Bamboo grove."

There the father ran and began to sought his child but didn't find her.

"O'Yone, O'Yone," he called out again and again.

He heard no answer and the dry wind sighed in the Bamboo leaves. Then he felt in his sleeves and brought forth the flute and after putting it to his lips heard a faint sighing sound.

"Father, dear father, my wicked stepmother killed me. Three moons since she killed me. She buried me in the clearing of the Bamboo Grove. You may find my bones there. As for me you will never see me anymore."

Hearing this with this two-handed sword he did justice and slew his wicked wife thus avenging the death of his innocent child. Then he dressed himself in a coarse white raiment with a great rice-straw hat, took a staff and a straw rain-coat, bound sandals on his feet and set forth upon a pilgrimage to the holy places of Japan.

And carried the little flute with him in a fold of his garment upon his breast.

The Boy who drew Cats

Once there was a boy who loved to draw and his name was Joji. He grew up on a farm with lots of brothers and sisters. The other children lent a helping hand to their parents but Joji was the only one who refused. He did nothing but enjoyed drawing on the dirt with a stick. And what Joji drew was only cats and nothing else.

His father warned him not to draw cats.

"Joji, you must stop drawing cats"

"I am sorry, father. I will stop."

But whenever Joji saw one of the farm cats go by, he forgot about his chores and started drawing cats.

"Joji will never make a farmer" said the farmer sadly to his wife.

"Maybe he could become a priest," she told him. "Why don't you take him to the temple?"

So, the farmer brought Joji to the temple to see the priest.

The priest said, "I will gladly teach him."

From then on Joji lived in the temple. The priest gave him lessons in reading and writing. Joji had his own box of writing tools, a brush, an ink stick and a stone.

Joji loved to make the ink. He poured water in the hollow of the stone, dipped the ink stick in the water and then rubbed the stick on the stone and thus made the ink for his brush.

The other students worked hard at their writing. But Joji with his brush and rice paper did nothing but draw. And what Joji drew was nothing but cats.

Cats, Cats and more Cats. Small Cats. Big Cats. Thin Cats.

Fat Cats. Cats, cats, cats, cats.

"Joji, the priest told him, "You must stop drawing cats. How will you be a priest?"

Joji gave the sand reply.

"I am sorry honorable sir, but I will stop."

And he did try but whenever he saw a cat pass by, he forgot about his writing and drew cats. If that was not bad enough, he started drawing cats on the walls of the temple. They were everywhere!

"Joji, you will never make a priest," the priest told him sadly." "You will have to go home."

Joji packed his bags but was afraid to go home because he knew his father would be angry.

Then he remembered a temple in the village nearby.

"Maybe I can stay with the priest there."

Joji started out walking but it was already night as he got to the other village. He climbed the steps to the other temple and knocked. There was no answer. He opened the heavy door. It was dark inside.

"That's strange," said Joji. "Why isn't anyone here?"

He lit a lamp by the door. Then he saw something which made him clap. All around the room were folding screens with empty rice paper panels.

Joji got his writing box out and made some ink. He dipped his brush and started to draw. And what Joji drew was one thing. Cats.

Cats, Cats, and more Cats. Small cats, big cats, thin cats, Fat Cats. Cats, Cats, Cats, Cats.

The last screen he drew on was as large as the room. Joji covered it with one gigantic cat--the biggest and most beautiful cat he had ever drawn.

Now Joji was tired and started to lie down. But something about the big room bothered him.

He found a cozy closet and settled inside. Then he shut the panel door and went to sleep. Late that night Joji was awakened in a fright.

He heard a sound. It sounded like a large fierce animal in the temple. He understood why the temple was empty and wished that he wasn't there either!

He heard the thing sniff around the big room and it halted right in front of the closet. Then all at once…..Yowl!

There was a sound of struggling and a roar of surprise and pain. Then there was a huge thud that shook the floor. Then a soft padding sound. Then silence.

Joji lay trembling in the dark. He stayed there for hours afraid to look out of the closet.

At last, daylight showed at the edge of the door. Joji slid the door open and peered out.

In the middle of the room lay a monster rat—a rat as big as a cow! It lay dead, as if something had smashed it to the floor.

Joji looked around the room. No one and nothing else was there--just the screens with the cats. Then Joji looked at the gigantic cat he had drawn.

"Didn't I draw the head to the left and tail to the right?"

Yes, he was sure of it. But now the cat faced the other way—as if it had come down off the day screen and then gone back up.

Joji grew pale. His eyes grew wide. Then he pressed his palms together and bowed to the screen.

"Thank You honorable cat. You have saved me. For as long as I live, no one will stop me from drawing cats."

When the villagers learned that the Monster rat was dead, Joji became a hero. The village priest let him live in the temple for as long as he liked.

Bur Joji didn't become a priest. And he didn't become a farmer.

He became an artist. A great artist. An artist honored all over the country. An artist who just drew one thing.

Cats!

The Wooden Bowl

Once upon a time there lived a couple who had seen better days. Formerly they were well to do for no fault of their own and in their old age they became so poor that they were just able to make ends and means.

One joy however remained to them. Their child. A good and gentle maiden of wonderful beauty and in all that land she had no equal.

At length the father fell sick and died and the mother and daughter had to work harder. Soon, the mother felt her strength weakening and was sad about leaving her daughter alone in this world.

The beauty of the maiden was so dazzling that it became the cause of much thought and anxiety to the dying mother. She gathered that it would prove to be a misfortune instead of a blessing.

Fearing her end to be near, her mother called the daughter to her bedside and with many words of love advised her to continue pure and be true to her soul.

Her beauty was a perilous gift which might become her ruin and commanded her to hide it as much as possible from the sight of men.

The mother placed on the head of her daughter a lacquered wooden bowl which she warned on all grounds never to take off. The bowl overshadowed the maidens face and it was impossible to tell the beauty hidden beneath it.

After her mother's death the poor child was rather forlorn. But she had a brave heart and at once set about earning her living in the fields by hard work.

As she was never seen without the wooden bowl which appeared to be a funny head dress she became the talk of the town and came to be known as the Maid with the bowl on her head.

Proud and bad people scorned at her and the idle young men of the village made fun of her and tried to pull it off her head.But it seemed to be permanently fixed and none of them succeeded in getting a glimpse of the beautiful face beneath.

The poor girl however was diligent in her work and crept quietly to her lonely home when the evening fell. Now, one day when she was at work in the field of a rich farmer who owned most of the land in that part drew near. He was struck by the modest behavior of the young girl and the diligence of her work and kept her in work till the end of the harvest. And winter came and took her to his own house to wait upon his wife who was bed sick.

Now the poor orphan had a happy home once more. She had become a child of the house rather than a servant.

After sometime the master's eldest son came to the house to visit his parents. He had been living in Kyoto, the rich city of Mikado where he had been learning and was glad to come back home. Week after week passed and to the surprise of his friends he showed no desire to return to the stirring life of the town.

No sooner had he set his eyes on the maiden with the wooden bowl on her head, he was filled with curiosity. He asked her who she was and why she never took off the unbecoming and strange head dress.

He was touched by her story and could not help laughing at her own fantasy. Day by day because of her goodness and gentle manners he laughed no more. And one day after having managed to take a peep under the bowl he saw enough of the beauty to make him fall deeply in love with her. From that moment he vowed to make the maiden with the wooden bowl his wife. His relations but would never hear of the match. They discussed that she was only a servant and so displayed such nice manners. She would one day turn against her benefactors and now their doubts were coming true and hated her wearing the ridiculous hat. It was doubtless to get a reputation for beauty which she most likely didn't possess. They were certain that she was plain looking.

The two old maiden aunts of the young man were bitter and never lost an opportunity of speaking unkind things about the poor orphan. Even her mistress who had been good to her turned against her and she had no friend left in the house except her master. The youngman however remained firm and considered his aunts as a pack of ill-natured inventions.

However, their opinions made him more steadfast and determined. A difficulty now arose. The poor little orphan had upset their calculations by refusing the hand of her master's son. They were angry at being made a bunch of fools by the girl.

The girl gradually noticed the cold looks her mistress and the people of the house gave her and what they meant even though they had sheltered her in her poverty. Rather than bring trouble in that happy home she chose to leave the house forever. She shed tears and remained true to her purpose. But that night her mother appeared in her dream and told her to yield to the prayers of her lover.

When the young man once more entreated her the next morning she gave a nod to the relationship. The members of the household were suspicious but the young man was too happy to mind them. The wedding day was fixed and grand celebrations were undergone. Still there were many unpleasant remarks made about the maid but the young man was adamant.

When the wedding day had come and all the people were assembled it became necessary to remove the wooden bowl from the head of the bride. The bride tried to take it off but to her dismay it got stuck and the utmost efforts of the relatives was also unsuccessful. However, the bridegroom consoled the maiden and insisted on continuing the ceremony without much ado.

The time came for the wine caps to be brought in and when the bride and bridegroom had to drink together to become man and wife.

Hardly had the bride put her lips to the cup. The wooden bowl burst open with a loud noise and fell to a thousand pieces on the floor. And with the bowl a shower of precious stones, pearls and diamonds, rubies and emeralds which had been hidden beneath it, besides gold and silver were found to the astonishment of the people who had assembled in the wedding.

Never was there such a merry wedding or such a lovely bride and such a proud and happy bridegroom.

Reflections

Long ago in the city of Kioto there lived a gentleman of good estate. His wife had been dead for many years and the good man lived in great peace and quiet with his only son and they always kept clear of womankind and knew nothing of their ways for they admired the cherry flower in the spring and later set out to view the Iris or the Lotus. And at these times they would drink and be as jolly as possible and twist their blue and white tenugui about their heads and often came home by the evening but wore their oldest clothes and were irregular in their meals.

The father soon felt the old age creeping on him. So, one night when they were warming their hands over charcoal, he announced to his son that he should get married soon.

The Young man cried, "What makes uou say such horrible things?"

"You must be joking."

"I am not joking," says the father.

"I never spoke a truer word and you will know soon enough"

"But father," replied the son

"I am mortally afraid of women."

"I am sorry for you my boy," says the father

"In the way of nature I am soon to die and you must find someone to take care of you."

Now, tears stood in the eyes of the youngman but he replied—

"I can take care of myself."

The long and short of it is that they found the youngman a wife. She was young and as pretty as a picture. Her name was Tassel or Fusa in her language.

They drank together three times three and became man and wife. The youngman now looking hard at the girl for he was afraid to converse with her took a bit of her sleeve and stroked it with his hand. The girl turned red, turned pale, turned red again and burst into tears.

The young man requested the maiden, "Please for the sake of honor don't cry."

But from then on they managed to get on pretty well and things were not as bad as they seemed. By and by the way of nature the old man died. He had left all his wealth to the young man. But this was no comfort to the poor youngman who mourned his father. Day and night he paid reverence to the tomb and got no or little sleep.

He gave little heed to his wife Mistress Tassel or even to the delicate dishes she set before him.

She said, "My dear and how would it be if you were to go to Kioto for a little?"

"And what should I do that for?" he says

"To enjoy yourself."

She immediately saw that it would never do to say that and kept quiet.

So, she says as a kind of duty– "Oh!"

"They say that every man who loves his country should visit Kioto; and besides l, you may give an eye to the fashions."

"To buy my things," she further prods.

"Are behind the times and I would like to know what people are wearing."

"I have no heart to go to Kioto," says the youngman.

"It is the planting time of rice and I have no heart to leave."

All the same he bids his wife farewell and gets out his best hakama and haori to make his bento for a journey.

"I am thinking of going to Kioto," he tells her.

"Well, I am surprised and if I may ask, what put such an idea into your head?" says the wife.

"I have been thinking and it is a duty," says the youngman.

To this Mistress Tassel said nothing more. And the next morning she packs her husband bright and early for Kioto.

The youngman steps down the road feeling a little better and in high spirits and it was not long before he reached Kioto.

He saw castles and gardens, and marched up and down fine streets of shops, gazing about him with his eyes wide open and his mouth too for he was a simple soul.

At length he came upon a shop full of metal mirrors that glittered in the sunshine.

He dared to pick up one of them thinking that it was a silver moon. The next moment he turned white as rice and sat on the door of the shop still holding the mirror in his hands and looking into it.

Perplexed, he enquired "Why father, how did you come here?"

You are not dead yet then?"

"Never mind, but you look pale and young."

"Your smile too is well."

"Fine mirrors, my young gentleman," said the shopman, "the best can be made, and that's one of the best of the lot you have there in your hand."

The youngman clutched his mirror tight and sat staring stupidly enough at it.

"How much?" he whispers.

"Is it for sale?"

"For sale it is indeed, most noble sirl," said the shopman, "and the price is a trifle, only two bu. It's almost giving it away I am, as you will understand."

"Two bu——only two bu! Now the gods be praised for this their Mercy!" cried the happy youngman.

Now it was the shopman who wished he had asked three bu or even five. All the same he put a good face upon it, and packed the mirror in a fine white box and tied it up with green cords.

"Father," said the young man after he had gotten away with it, "before we set out for home we must buy some for my wife, you know."

When he came to his home the young man never said a word to Mistress Tassel about buying his old father for two bu in the Kioto shop. As things turned out that was where he made the mistake.

Mistress Tassel was pleased with her coral hair-pins and her fine new obi from Kioto.

"I am glad to see him well and so happy."

"But men are just like children."

As for her husband, unbeknown to her he took a bit of green silk from her treasure box and spread it in the cupboard of the toko no ma. There he placed the mirror in its box of white wood.

Every early morning and every late evening, he went to the cupboard of the toko no ma and spoke with his father. Many a jolly talk they had and many a hearty laugh together and the son was the happiest young man of all that countryside, for he was a simple soul.

But Mistress Tassel had a quick eye and sharp ear and it was not long before she understood her husband's new ways.

"What for does he go so often to the toko no ma," she asked herself, "and what has he got there? I should be glad enough to know." Not being one to suffer much in silence she very soon asked her husband the same things.

"H'mm," she says.

"And wasn't two bu cheap," he says, "and wasn't it a strange thing altogether?"

"Cheap Indeed," says she, "and passing strange; and why, if I may ask," she says, "did you say nothing of all this at the first?"

"I am sorry but I don't know," and with that went to his work.

Up jumped Mistress Tassel the minute he had turned his back and went to the toko no ma and flung open the doors.

She opened the box there quickly. Taking up the mirror in her hands for a moment she said nothing but great tears of anger and jealousy stood in her pretty eyes making her flush.

"A Woman!" she cried.

"So.that is his secret!"

"He keeps a woman in the cupboard who is so very pretty but no not so pretty but a dancing girl from Kioto!"

Ah, who could have thought it of him?"

"I am a miserable girl....I am!"

"—---and I have cooked his daikon and mended his hakama a hundred times. Oh! Oh!"

With that she threw the mirror into its case and slammed the cupboard door upon it. She flung upon the mat herself and cried and sobbed and cried.

In comes her husband.

In an instant he was on his knees beside Mistress Tassel doing what he could do to comfort her and to get her face up from the floor where she kept it.

"Why, what is it, my own darling?" he says.

"Your own darling!" she answers fiercely.

"But,my sweet you are at home,and with your husband"

"Pretty husband!," she says

"And pretty going ons with a woman in a cupboard."

At that she jumped to her feet and danced with rage.

"Old father! old father! old father!" she screamed: "am I a fool or a child? I saw the woman with my own eyes."

The poor young man was head over heels. He took the mirror from the toko no ma.

"It is my father," said the young man.

"I bought him in Kioto for two bu."

"He keeps a woman in the cupboard who has stolen my green sleeve-linings," sobbed the wife.

After this there was a great to-do. Some of the neighbors took the man's part and some the woman's, with such clatter and chatter and noise as never was; but settle the thing they could not, and none of them would look into the mirror, because they said it was bewitched.

They might have gone on their way but one of them said, "Let us ask Lady Abbess, for she is a wise woman."

And off they all went to do what they might have done sooner.

The Lady Abbess was a pious young woman, the head of a convent of holy nuns. She was the great one at prayers and meditations and at mortifying the flesh, and she was the clever one, nonetheless at human affairs. They took her to the mirror and she held it in her hands and looked into it for a long time and spoke at last.

"This poor woman," she said touching the mirror, "for it is as plain as daylight that it is a woman—this poor woman was so troubled in her mind at the disturbance that she caused a quiet house, that she has taken vows, shaved her head and become a holy nun. Thus, she is in her right place here. I will keep her, and instruct her in prayers and meditation. Go home, my children; forgive and forget, be friends."

Then all the people said, "The Lady Abbess is the wise woman."

And she kept the mirror in her treasure.

Mistress Tassel and her husband went home hand in hand.

"So, I was right, you see, after all," she said.

"Yes, yes, my dear," said the simple young man, "Of course. But I was wondering how my old father would get on at the holy convent. He was never much of a one for religion."

The Good Thunder

Folk tales tell us that the Thunder, Rai-den is an unloving spirit, revengeful and cruel to man. There are people who are afraid of the storm, lighting and tempest and know Rai-den and his son Rai-Taro to be evil entities but maybe they are wrong.

Rai-den lived in a castle of clouds set high in the blue heaven and was a great God, a Lord of the elements and Rai-Taro was his only son, a very brave boy and was the darling child of his father.

During the evening both father and son walked upon the ramparts of the castle of cloud and from there could look down upon the men and women of the Reed Plains navigating the north east, west including the south and very often but not so often laughed at the people below sometimes expressing a sigh or a concern at times. Rai-Taro would sometimes lean further more towards the edge and could thus get a glimpse of the children scuttling to and fro upon the earth.

From the northern part they looked and could see men at arms going to battle. From the southern part they looked and could see priests serving in the temples where the air was dim with incense and images of gold and bronze danced in the twilight. From the eastern ramparts they looked and could observe a fair princess and a troop of maidens clad in rose color and made music for her. There were also children there playing with a little cart of flowers.

"Ah! the pretty children!" exclaimed Rai-Taro.

From the western ramparts they looked and could see a peasant toiling in a rice-field who was very weary with a back ache. The Peasants were poor and wore ragged clothes.

"Have they no children?" asked Rai-Taro.

Rai-den shook his head.

"Have you looked very well, Rai-Taro?"

"Have you looked this night upon the doings of men?"

"Father," said Rai-Taro, "indeed I have looked well."

"Then choose, my son, choose, for I send you to take up habitation upon the earth."

"Must I go among men?" asked Rai-Taro

"My child, you must."

"I will not go north to the men at arms for fighting makes me very ill."

"Oho, say you so, my son? Will you go, then, to the Fair Lady's bower?"

"No," said Rai-Taro, "I am a Man. Neither will I have my head shaved or go to live with the priests."

"What, then, do you choose the poor peasant? You will have a hard life, Rai-Taro"

Rai-Taro said, "They have no children and perhaps they will love me."

"Go, go in peace," said Rai-den; "For you have chosen wisely."

"How shall I go, my father?" said Rai-Taro

"Honorably as it befits the Prince of the heavens"

Now the poor peasant who toiled in his field which sat at the foot of the mountain Hakusan in the province of Ichizen. Day after day the bright sun shone making up the place. So, the field was dry and the rice burnt up.

"Alack and alas," cried the peasant "and what shall I do if my rice crops fail?"

May the dear gods have mercy on the poor people!"

With that he sat himself down on a stone and fell asleep.

When he woke up the sky was black with clouds. It was noon but it grew as dark as night. The leaves of the tree shuddered together and the birds stopped singing.

Cried the peasant, "Rai-den is going out on his black horse and we shall have plenty of rain, Thanks be."

Sure, enough there was rain and it fell in torrents, with blinding lighting and roaring thunder.

"Oh, Rai-Den," said the peasant, "saving your greatness, this is more than sufficient."

At this fell to the earth a living ball of fire and the heavens crackle with a mighty peal of thunder.

"Ai, Ai," cried the poor peasant man thinking that the Thunder dragon would take him down.

However, the thunder dragon spared him.

And soon he sat and rubbed his eyes. The ball of fire was gone and instead a baby lay upon the wet earth. A fine fresh boy was with the rain upon his cheeks and hair.

"This is sweet mercy," cried the peasant and carried the baby home.

As he went the sun came out on the blue sky and every flower in the cooler air shone and lifted up its head.

"What may it be?" asked his wife.

The man answered, "Rai-Taro, the little eldest son of the thunder."

Rai-Taro grew up straight and strong. He was the delight of his foster parents and all the neighbors loved him. When he was ten years old, he worked in the rice fields like a man. He was the wonderful weather prophet.

He decided, "Let us do this or that for we shall have fair weather."

And whatever he said, so sure enough it came to pass. And he brought great good fortune to the poor peasant man and all his works prospered.

When Rai-Taro was eighteen years old all the neighbors were invited to the birthday feast. There was plenty of good food and the folk made merry. Only Rai-Taro was silent and sorry.

"What ails you, Rai-Taro?" said husband foster mother

"You who want to be the gayest of the gay, why are you so silent, sad and sorry?"

"It is because I must leave you," Rai-Taro said.

"Never leave us," Rai-Taro, my son. Why would you leave us?"

"Mother, because I must," said Rai-Taro in tears.

"You have been our good fortune; you have given us all things. What have I given you Rai-Taro my son?"

Rai-Taro answered, "Three things you have taught me—to labor, to suffer and to love. I am more learned than immortals."

Then he went from them. And in the likeness of a white cloud he scaled heaven's blue height till he gained his father's castle. And Raiden received him. The two of them stood on the western ramparts of the Castle of Cloud and looked down to earth.

The foster mother stood weeping bitterly with the husband holding her hand.

A Legend of Kwannon

In the days of gods, Ama-no-Hashidate was the Floating Bridge of heaven by which the deities came from heaven to earth bearing their jewels, spears, magic mirrors and wonder robes. After which it was closed and the deities never bothered to come to earth. The people still named a place Ama-no-Hashidate on earth for the sake of Happy memory. This place is one of the Three Fair Views of Yamato. It is where a strip of land runs out to the sea.

There was a holy man of Kioto called Saion Zenji who has followed the way of the gods right from his youth. He was a disciple of Buddha well versed in philosophy and knew the perils of illusion and the ineffable joys of Nirvana. He would spend his day meditating and knew many scriptures by heart. When he was on a pilgrimage he came across the floating bridge. He offered to the place a note of thanks for the place that was lovely to his eyes.

"The blind and ignorant have it that trees and rocks and the green water are not sentient things but here I will take up my rest and join my voice with theirs and will not see my house again."

The holy Man thus climbed to the top of the mountain set against the Ama-no-Hashidate and when he reached the place called Lone Pine built himself a shrine to worship Kwannon the Merciful and a hut to cover his own head.

All day he chanted the holy sutras from dawn to eventide singing till his very being seemed to float in an ecstacy of praise and his voice majestic and loud it was till the blue Campanula of the mountain bowed its head, the great white lily distilled incense from its heart, the cicala shrieked aloud and the forsaken bird gave a long nod from the thicket.

Around the hermit's hut fluttered dragon-flies and butterflies innumerable which are of course a symbol of the happy dead. In the valleys peasant people were comforted in their toil, the sun and wind were tempered and the rain fell softly upon their faces. These people climbed the mountain to kneel at the shrine of Kwannon the Merciful, and to speak with the holy man whose wooden bowl they filled with rice or millet or barley-meal or beans. Sometimes the holy man visited the nearby villages and soothed the sick and blessed the children.

Now in that country comes the winter season. First came the wild wind of the north and then came the snow in great flakes for a period of nine days. The folks kept in the valley kept warm as they could but the cold was bitter. At the Lone Pine the snow was piled and drifted and the shrine could not be seen anymore. The holy man lived upon the food that was in the bowl for a while but after that passed many days in meditation which was like meat, drink and sleep to him but at length all the men in the valley trembled with bodily weakness.

"Forgive me, O Kwannon the Merciful," said Zenji; "but it seems to me that if I have no food I die."

Turning he beheld a dappled hind lying on the snow, dead because of the cold.

"Poor gentle creature, never more shalt thou run in the hills and nibble the grass and flowers."

He went on, "Isn't it forbidden by the law of the blessed one? Is it not forbidden by the word of Kwannon the Merciful?"

But even as he mused, he heard voice that said:

"Alas! If thou die of hunger and cold, what shall become of the people of the valley? Shall they be condemned without you chanting the sutras of the Tathagata? Break the law to keep the law though that countest the world is well lost without a divine song?"

Then presently Zenji took a knife out and cut him a piece of flesh from the dappled hind. He gathered fir cones and made fire and cooked the deer's flesh in an iron pot and ate all of it. And his strength came to him again and he opened his lips and sang praises to the Tathagata and the embers of the dying fire leapt up to hear him.

"I must bury the poor deer," said Zenji.

So, he went to the door of his hut but could find no deer nor dappled hinds nor the mark of it on snow.

"It is strange," wondered Zenji.

As soon as the wind reduced the people of the valley came to see how the hermit had fared.

"The gods he is not dead of cold or hunger."

But they found him chanting in his hut and he told them how he had eaten the flesh of a deer.

"I cut but a small portion of the meat and kept it in an iron pot," recalled the holy man.

But when they came to look, they found no flesh nor deer but a piece of cedar wood gilded upon the one side. Marveling deeply, they carried it to the shrine of Kwannon the Merciful and clearing away the deep snow sat down to worship. There smiled the image of the sweet heavenly lady, golden among the golden flowers. In her right side there was a gash where the gilded wood was cut. The poor folk brought what was in the pot and set it in the gash. And immediately the wound was healed and smooth gold shone over the place. All the people fell on their faces but the hermit stood singing the high praise of Kwannon the Merciful.

The sun set in glory and the folk crept softly from the shrine and went to their homes. The cold moon and stars shone upon the Lone Pine and the Floating Bridge and the Sea.

Through a rent in the roof of the shrine they illuminated the face of Kwannon the Merciful and made visible her manifold arms of love. Yet Zenji, her servant, stood before her singing in ecstasy with tears upon his face.

"O wonder-woman, strong and beautiful Tender-hearted, pitiful thousand-armed! Thou hast fed me with thine own flesh—Mystery of mysteries! In the deep of my own heart to keep yet break thy law—Kwannon the Merciful lady, stay with me, save me from her perils of illusion; Let me not be afraid of the snow or the Lone Pine. Mystery of mysteries— Thou hast refused Nirvana, Help me that I may lose the world, content, And sing the Divine Song."

The Goblin of Adachigahara

Long long ago in the province of Mutsu in Japan there was a large plain called Adachigahara. This place was haunted by a cannibal goblin who took the form of an old woman. The old women and girls who were at work at the wells whispered dreadful stories of how the missing folk had been lured to the goblins cottage and were eaten alive for the goblin liked to devour human flesh. No one dared to venture near the haunted spot after sunset and the travelers also kept away from the dreaded place.

One day a priest came to the plain. He was a Buddhist pilgrim wearing sacred robes who walked from shrine to shrine to ask for blessings. He had lost his way and met no one who could warn him about the haunted spot.

It was late Autumn and the evenings were chilly and the priest was tired and hungry and was lost in the plain and looked about in vain for some human habitation. At last he saw a clump of trees and through the branches caught a single ray of light escaping from the space in between which brought him immense joy.

He thought to himself, " Surely, I will get a night's lodging in the cottage."

He dragged his weary feet towards the spot and came to the cottage which was miserable looking. As he drew near, he saw that the cottage needed repairs. The fence was broken and weeds were growing in the garden pushing themselves through the gaps. The paper screen which served as windows was full of holes. The posts of the house scarcely supported the thatched roof. He could by the light of an old lantern make out an old woman who was industriously spinning.

The pilgrim called out to her, "I am a traveler, O' old woman and have nowhere to rest for the night. I beg you to let me spend the night here."

The old woman as soon as she heard the priest stopped spinning, rose from her seat and approached him.

"I am very sorry for you. You must be very tired. Unfortunately, I have no bed to offer you and cannot put up with you."

"Oh, that does not matter," said the priest; "all I want is some kind of shelter and I was hoping that you would be good enough to let me sleep on the kitchen floor otherwise I will have to sleep out on the cold plain."

"Very well, I will let you stay here but can offer you only a poor welcome. Come and I will light the fire for you," condensed the old woman.

"You must be very hungry after a long journey. I will cook supper for you."

She then went to the kitchen to cook some rice.

After the priest had finished his supper, the old woman sat down by the fireplace and they talked for a long time.

Soon, the fire died down and the priest was shivering.

"I see that you are cold," said the old woman.

"I will go gather some wood, but you must take care of the house while I am gone."

The pilgrim replied, "Let me go instead for you are old."

The old woman shook her head and said:

"You must stay quietly here, for you are my guest."

In a minute she came back and said:

"You must sit where you are and be careful not to move or go near and look into the inner room."

The old woman then went out again and the priest was left alone. The only light in the hut was from the dim lantern and the words of the woman had now aroused in him a fear. The priest was curious.

But the promise he had given came back to him and after sometime could no longer resist his curiosity to peep into the forbidden place.

He got up and began to move slowly towards the back room. But then he thought that the old woman would be angry with him and again came back to the fireside.

As the time passed slowly the priest could not contain his curiosity.

"She will not know that I looked unless I tell her."

With these words he got up and crept towards the forbidden spot. With trembling hands, he pushed back the sliding door and looked in. What he saw froze the blood in his veins. The room was full of flesh and bones and the walls were splashed and the floor was covered with blood. The smell of the decaying flesh made him faint.

He moved backwards in fear and lay in a pitiful heap on the floor. His teeth chattered and he could hardly crawl away from the dreadful spot.

He cried out, "May Buddha help me or I am lost."

He ran as fast his legs could carry him and he ran out in the night as far away as possible from the goblins' haunt.

He had not gone far when he heard steps behind him and a voice crying: "Stop! Stop!"

The priest quite forgot how tired he was and flew over the ground faster than ever for he knew that if the goblin caught him, he would soon be one of her victims.

He prayed to Buddha:

"Namu Amida Butsu, Namu Amida Butsu."

And after him rushed the dreadful old hag, her hair flying in the wind. In her hand she carried a large blood stained knife and shrieked after him to stop.

At last, when the priest felt that he could run no more the dawn broke, and with this the goblin vanished and he was safe.

The priest now knew that he had met the goblin of Adachigahara, the story of whom he had often heard but never believed to be true. He felt that he owed his wonderful escape to the protection of the Buddha to whom he had prayed for help. So, he took out his rosary and bowed his head as the sun rose and said his prayers again earnestly.

He then set forward for another part of the country, only too glad to leave the haunted plain behind him.

About the Author

Priyanka Bhandarkar

Priyanka Bhandarkar has completed her post-graduation in English literature from the Karnataka State Open University. She has dared to follow her dreams and is the Co-Author of 120+ Anthologies and Author of Seven Solo Books which are a collection of poetry available on Amazon. Taking inspiration from the words of Thomas Edison, she believes that there is no substitute for hard work.

You Can Reach Her Here:

Mail—*Priyankabhandarkar18@gmail.com*

Instagram *@poet_and_poems*

www.ingramcontent.com/pod-product-compliance
Lightning Source LLC
LaVergne TN
LVHW041617070526
838199LV00052B/3180